The Dust of Mars

The Dust of Mars

Harry Cobb Series

Robert P. Fitton
Author of over 30 books across the genres.

iUniverse, Inc.
New York Lincoln Shanghai

The Dust of Mars
Harry Cobb Series

iUniverse books may be ordered through booksellers or by contacting:

iUniverse
2021 Pine Lake Road, Suite 100
Lincoln, NE 68512
www.iuniverse.com
1-800-Authors (1-800-288-4677)

ISBN: 978-0-595-48534-5 (pbk)
ISBN: 978-0-595-60629-0 (ebk)

Printed in the United States of America

CHAPTER 1

Despite his lack of character Jason Rapp did not deserve a death sentence. I had enjoyed a pleasant shuttle flight from Orbitus to Mars until Rapp's call rattled my zip connection. The wind howled and sand grains pattered against his rover's bubble top, suggesting a severe dust storm. He said someone in a silver terrain suit, brandishing a pinpoint pulser, had hiked through the Martian ridge shadows. Rapp sensed murderous intent.

At first I wanted to chide him for not meeting me for breakfast on Orbitus. Just ten hours ago, he slipped me important information, coinciding with my trip to Mars, about a cover-up in the Turcotte ore refining operation on the planet. The security chief for the Turcotte operation told me the same thing, but my attention was now directed toward Rapp's pleas for help.

As the pinpoint was aimed at the bubble he frantically described the tinted face shield of his potential killer. Twenty-five years at the Space Investigative Bureau alerted me to the shrill crescendo of a pinpoint pulser's thin red beam. I heard the bubble rip as Rapp cried out for mercy. The outward gush of air into the cold, diminished Martian atmosphere was soon replaced by his mournful whimper. He pushed out my name in his last remaining gasps. "*Cobb ...*"

"Rapp, Rapp can you hear me?" I sat up fully in the recliner and gripped my perforated zip. The signal went out. "Rapp!"

The pulverizing sand and wind gusts were louder now. I leaned toward the shuttle's oval portal. Behind the backdrop of stars, Mars cast a rusty glow beyond the shuttle's gray wing. Rapp was dead thousands of kilometers away on the planet's surface.

I flipped up the recliner tray as images of Rapp in his dark tuxedo at Orbitus's black jack tables shot through my brain like bursts from the pinpoint. My shoes connected to the floor forces and I started down the aisle. The forward hatch was sealed.

One of the attendants, an affable young woman with bouncy blonde hair, stared from the adjacent alcove and flashed her white teeth before she spoke. "Mr. Cobb, if you're looking for the bathroom, it's to the rear of this section."

"I need to speak with the navigator," I said brusquely.

"The navigator?" she asked as if the question had transcended her usual answers about food, drink or rester pillows. "I don't understand."

"Miss, I'm a private investigator, former SIB agent. One of my clients is in trouble on the planet. I need the navigator's assistance."

"Yes, of course."

I removed my license, retired bureau disks, and placed them in her smooth palm. "Let the pilot check these."

She squinted, seemed confused, but complied with my request. Her long red fingernails tapped out a code on the side panel. The hatch slid open and remained open as she walked down a narrow corridor. Silhouetted cabin figures were positioned in front of glowing console panel lights and the encroaching, brown Martian sphere. I glanced briefly at the hint of upper ice caps as I exhaled.

The attendant leaned over a man seated at a darkened alcove containing numerous window monitors. She held out her hand and pointed toward me as she spoke. The man glanced at me and took both disks from her hand. I could see him lean over one of the window screens. Then he nodded and waved me up front. I checked my zip window, now set to standard time at the Livingston Dome. It was 1:44 PM.

I squeezed my large frame through the hatch and moved sideways down the connector corridor. The young man stood in his light blue neck liner and dark pants. He extended his hand quickly and I wondered if he approved of my long bureau record. "Mr. Cobb, what can I do for you?"

I studied his black name badge embroidered into his neck liner at the shoulder. "Moss … I need an enhanced scan of the planet's surface. I just received a distress call from a potential informant and think he's been murdered." I handed him my zip.

"Last call coordinates are locked in my zip memory."

Moss nodded once and positioned my zip on his station counter. He immediately hooked in a relay, punched a few buttons on the panel, and a Mercator map of Mars appeared on his window monitor. A green dot flashed in the northern hemisphere, center of the Elysium Planitia. I recognized the area because it was my destination. Moss looked up. "He's eighteen kilometers out from the Livingston Dome. On Turcotte land … Looks like there is an industrial plant five kilometers back and another twelve kilometers ahead. Actual heading is: thirty-five point two north and one hundred and eight west longitude."

"I was afraid of that."

"What do you mean?" asked Moss.

"Ongoing investigation, son. Can you bring me an image from the signal's center?"

"That will not be a problem, sir."

"Excellent." As he worked the panels under the huge window monitor, I unclipped my zip and placed a call to Jahn Patenaude in Livingston's security office.

Moss now had a full picture of Mars and he adjusted the clarity as my zip buzzed. After a brief rustling on the other end, Pate-naude's raspy voice came over my zip speaker. "Jahn Patenaude."

"Jahn, this is Harry."

"Harry, my boy … Calling to put in your dinner menu at the Excelsior?"

"They know what I like. Jahn, we have a problem the other side of IP-5. Twelve kilometers toward IP-7."

Patenaude cleared his throat and his voice assumed its professional, authoritative tone. "What happened?"

"Guy named Jason Rapp. He has info on problems at IP-5. Somebody just shot a pinpoint at him through his rover bubble."

"Poppycock."

"I'm not kidding, Jahn. You need to get somebody out there."

"*Really …*"

"The navigator has the area on screen. Bad dust storm."

Moss reduced the screen to a current six hundred square kilometer resolution. The Livingston Dome and smaller surrounding support domes were clear, but across the brown, rock strewn, crater punched desert, a wispy gray dust cloud, measuring several hundred kilometers back, swirled toward IP-5 and support domes. Tracking a potential killer was now impossible.

I heard Patenaude calling troopers on another zip. Then he came back on my zip connection. "Harry, I can visibly see that storm?"

"The rover site is in the thick of it."

"Listen, I'll request Kranz and some troopers head into that storm."

"Kranz?" I grit my teeth. Kranz was an obnoxious, power hungry puppet of Norman Burkhart. As Livingston's security chief Burkhart was bought and paid for by the Turcottes. "Does it have to be Kranz?"

"He's the only one crazy enough to fly out there in a dust storm ... Besides you and me."

I thought back to the numerous times Kranz had interfered with my investigations both with the bureau and after I retired. "Whatever. You'd better call Ed Stanton, too. He's the Turcotte security chief. Let him know what's going on."

"I'll call him. Look, you and I will trace the IP-7-Living-ston Road."

"What, from thirty-thousand feet.?" I asked as Moss scanned the storm edges. Readings showed the dust had advanced another kilometer toward Livingston.

"This is a bad storm," said Moss.

Patenaude cleared his throat. "Harry, I'll meet you at the port. What is your ETA?"

"Four twenty-five," said Moss.

"I heard him," said Patenaude. "I'm also going to try and get a security satellite image. Maybe we can get scans through that storm."

"Brief me, I'm not going anywhere." I shut off the zip and turned to Moss. "Thanks for your help, Captain."

"Anytime, sir. We'll let you know if the storm clears."

After thanking both Moss and the attendant and I retreated down the corridor. I glanced at the packed shuttle, sat in the recliner and folded my arms across my chest. Last night was a night of hope and promise. When I wandered from my hotel room into the Orbitus casinos, I saw Ariana Cervantes' fluffy dark hair and deep eyes. She sipped the contents of a thin glass at the restaurant overlooking the gambling floor. My stomach tingled and I stalled above the gambling hall. No friend or foe could thrill me so quickly and so fully.

I leaned on the brass railing, amidst a plethora of conversation, crashing slot machine levers, black jack callers, and music. She tilted her head back slightly and with a gracious smile, seemed amused by her young dinner companion. Even from across the floor, her skin was luminous, and gold rings, gaping with colorful gems, adorned her fingers. Ten years had passed since we spent four days alone in the Barsoom Dome along the Valles Marineris canyons.

My professional instinct, responsible for rational decisions during my career with the bureau, held me back, but a romantic flair, filled with desire and intense longing, pushed me forward. I descended the stairs onto the smooth green gambling room carpet and stepped between the slot machines. The men and woman strenuously shifted the slot machine levers, but I focused on Ariana's wide cheekbones and stunning brown eyes. I cautioned myself against approaching this woman whom I deemed above me in class and breed.

Near the blackjack table a tall, handsome man and maybe ten years younger than me, handed over a wad of blue droits to the caller. Frustration revealed itself in the hardening crevice developing down his sloping forehead. His huge fists were closed and he shook his head as he turned.

"Damn," he said loud enough for me to hear him.

His blue eyes brightened, he pointed and called out my name through the crowd noise, but I didn't know him. I pretended not to hear him and eyed Ariana, now enjoying a colorful sherbet at the upper table. He finally reached me and grabbed my arm as I passed the table. I looked down at his hand as he breathed rapidly. "You're Harry Cobb."

"And who the hell are you?" I asked, my heart still beating fast in anticipation of seeing Ariana again.

His teeth were straight and white. "A man who can help you."

"I don't like riddles, mister," I told him. "Who are you?"

"Jason Rapp." He shook my hand, tightly as if he were holding on for comfort. "Stanton called you to check the Turcotte iron smelting plant."

"Ya, so what?"

"I know the truth about what really happened in that plant over the last year."

I raised my brows, viewing Ariana out of the corner of my eye. "And what, pray-tell is that?"

Confidence left his face and his teeth chaffed his lips. "I can't do that right now."

"You're wasting my time," I said and started across the floor again.

"Wait, there are financial considerations here."

"You just lost a full wad of droits." I said and faced him squarely.

"Listen, Stanton is concerned product was not properly manufactured, but he can't prove anything because it happened months ago."

"What?"

Rapp rubbed his mouth. "Look, Cobb. Meet me in the breakfast room here in the hotel. What time are you on?"

"Livingston Standard." I gave him my zip address. His shifting eyes indicated a man under pressure. He told me to meet him at seven a.m. and then bolted back to the gaming tables.

I alternated glances between Ariana and Rapp, and continued across the room. Less than fifty feet above me, Ariana sat in a sleeveless blue velvet dress and her layered dark hair was nestled on her bare shoulders. Again, I wanted to flee to the hotel shops, but instead, trudged up the marble staircase's oriental runner. I slowly rose above the leafy plants atop the retaining wall. Within the aromatic cuisine, the small restaurant's patrons were isolated within a cone of soft classical music, clean air, and sensual red light.

I reached the upper level. Ariana slowly lowered her glass when she saw me. The young man held her wrist as he turned. She set her glass on the table linen and stood. Her friend watched her saunter around the restaurant tables. She was not a tall woman, but had a slim waste and well defined figure, accentuated by the form fitting dress to the knee. Her lips parted and brown eyes filled as she extended her hands. Then she hugged me. "God, I thought I would never see you again, Harry."

Her sensual perfume and warm touch brought me back to the chateau inside the Barsoom Dome. I remembered nestling against her smooth white skin as the warm breezes wafted through the chateau. "Why did you leave, Ariana?"

"Some things are better left in the past." Her eyes brightened as she smiled. "But you're here now."

"I saw you from across the floor."

She looped her arm under my arm. "And you fought the urge all the way across the floor."

"Maybe …" I was fixed on her alluring, dark eyes. "You look just *wonderful …*"

She walked me to a brass railing above the gaming tables. "I often think of that time at Barsoom. I don't think I've ever felt so far away. Leaving my whole life somewhere else."

She kept her arm locked. Her touch was warm and charged my body with just an inkling of the thrill I experienced ten years ago. "Let me guess: as usual you are here on business."

"I am."

"I was sorry to hear about the death of your father. He founded an empire in Amalgamated Sureties."

Moisture glazed her eyes and her arm tightened. "Father, died before his time. None of us expected it."

"I was always amazed at how he inspired his people. I heard the pep talks. He was the main speaker the night we met."

"People, when properly following instructions, are the heart and soul of any operation." She turned like a window scanner slowly panning, released her arm, but held my hands. "I want to go out. Find a quiet place away from the fray and talk about old times."

"What about your dinner date?"

"You're my dinner date. What do you say?"

I kicked myself for having doubts when I earlier crossed the gambling floor. Her presence before me seemed like a dream.

"Sure."

Chapter 2

I opened my eyes when my zip sounded. The fuzzy window image revealed I had slept on the shuttle for nearly two hours. I sat up in the recliner, tightened my brow and lifted the zip to my ear. "Cobb, "I said in a low voice.

"Is that you, Harry?"

"Desmond?" I expected somebody had apprised the eldest Turcotte about the trouble in the desert between his two industrial plants.

"Harry, I have to tell you I am not a happy man at this moment."

I was fully awake now. "I'm sorry to hear that."

"While I support Ed Stanton asking for help, I am outraged that you chose not to notify me you were involved in the investigation at IP-5!"

"Oh?"

"No mind."

"Ed only told me someone is responsible for what he called in mess up in production. I—"

"Well, Ed should mind his own business," stated Desmond.

"He's your head of security."

"I offered you that position," said Desmond. "I want to know exactly what you have found out in your investigation."

"Absolutely nothing. Ed called me and I moved up my trip from next week to this week. I'm a consultant with my own clients."

"I don't want to hear a list of your accolades, Harry old boy." I was a little upset Desmond referred to me as old. "You tell me right now what you know."

"The dead man, Rapp, had information for me, but dead men make lousy informants."

"He's dead on my property. Security forces are all over the place!"

"Who is the plant engineer at IP-5?" I asked.

"Joe Lockheed. Don't be sticking your nose into places you shouldn't."

"What are you worried about?" I asked and awaited more cackle. "Burkhart does you bidding."

"There's a storm going on here. When it clears I'll have my men bring me out."

"Then you don't think Rapp's death has anything to do with what he knew about IP-5?" I asked.

"What did he tell you? If you're holding back …"

"I know as much as you do … But I plan to find out a whole lot more."

After a pause the frequency disconnected. I created a memo to Sadie on my zip. I wanted Renie, Max, and Jody made aware of Rapp's murder and I needed a background check on him. I stood and stretched in the aisle. Fatigue now followed me like a weight strapped to my back. When I was younger, I could easily survive on an hour's sleep. I trudged to the forward cabin and spotted the attendant checking packages in the stow compartments. "Mr. Cobb, I was going to wake you. Captain Moss has additional images from the surface."

"Bless you. I guess I needed my beauty sleep."

"I think anyone approaching forty needs more sleep."

I smiled and squeezed her wrist. "Bless you. Approaching forty. Thank you."

She smiled, raised her brows and opened the hatch. I was in the corridor before the door slid all the way back. I didn't see Moss at his console, but he soon appeared up front. He briefly introduced me to the pilot and the rest of the crew. Then he sat me in front of his window screen. The pictures from the surface, although recorded, were more detailed than a few hours ago. Utilizing reconnaissance satellites, Moss had captured a blurred depiction of a careened rover near a crater ravine.

"Scans indicate the bubble was pierced."

"That would coincide with what Rapp told me."

Later frames showed the arrival of tracers in the sky and crews had constructed a small, white containment dome around the rover.

"By the way," said Moss. "Inspector Patenaude from the Livingston Dome has contacted us three times. I told him you were sleeping."

"Bad habit, sleeping," I said and Moss smiled perfunctorily. "Is he still at Livingston?"

"He is. I believe at the port," said Moss as a frequency address appeared in the lower corner of the screen. "You can use this station if you wish."

"Thanks."

Moss accessed the address and handed me the station zip. I stared at the rover and the rounded dome base on the zip window as the frequency connected. "Jahn Patenaude."

"Jahn, it's Harry."

"Ah, the old man awakes from his afternoon nap."

"What is this with the old remarks?" Anyone else would have upset me with the quip. "You're as old as I am, gramps." "Touché."

"Fifty-two years does not qualify either of us for the dust bin." I thought back to last night when I walked Ariana into a quiet cafe away from the gambling floor. "What do you have on the Rapp thing, Jahn?"

"Kranz confirms what you said about the pinpoint pulser. Directly through the rover bubble. Rapp was not wearing a terrain suit or any protection. Wouldn't have done him a damn bit of good. He bled to death inside that rover. Everything was frozen."

"What about the area around the rover?" I asked and continued to study the screen image from half an hour ago.

"With that wind? Are you kidding? Everything is wiped clean. We got the satellite images and relayed them to Moss up there. There was a gap of fifty-three minutes to get through channels. More than enough time for anybody to leave the murder scene."

"That's not good. The killer had fifty-three minutes to escape."

"Over an hour until we had scans of the connector roads," said Patenaude. "I had roads blocked to Livingston, but with that storm, anyone with a decent rover could have looped around and then continued. I have a report pending on all rented rovers and rovers leaving the Livingston exit gates over the past twenty-four hours."

"Unless the killer didn't come from Livingston." I nodded and sat down again. "Jahn, Desmond called me on the zip. He is not too happy."

"Tell me about it. He is demanding my office inform him about what we know about the IP-5 problem. I don't know what the hell he's talking about."

I cleared my throat. "Apparently, this IP-5 thing is bigger than Ed or any of us thought. Listen, Jahn, my zip has a playback of the attack."

"And?"

"I'm concerned about the pinpoint pulse frequency. I'll memo the playback to you and the bureau can trace the manufacturer."

"That was my next request, sir. Now get your rump down here and we'll take a little trip into the desert."

"Will do. Cobb out." I looked up from the rover scan and then into Moss's blue eyes. "Captain, again, thank you for your help here."

"Any time, Commander," said Moss with a quirky grin.

"Ah, you checked my bureau record."

"Yes, sir. Standard procedure—"

"No need to explain, Captain," I said as I stood and patted him on the back. "I'll be back in my recliner if anything else comes in."

"Understood," he said as I turned, "Sir."

"I'm retired," I said halfway down the corridor. I admired Moss's thoroughness and ability to follow regulations. I grinned at the attendant and returned to my recliner.

I plugged the zip into the recliner window and immediately accessed the plea from Rapp, captured only two hours ago. After memoing Patenaude, I pushed the playback. Rapp made no mention of any suspicions about his assailant nor did he provide any description other than someone in a t-suit, wielding a pinpoint. His wails and the ensuing high-pitched pinpoint prompted me to close the zip.

I thought about checking his background myself, but shut down the zip window. Sadie was a proficient coordinator and would provide me with a complete check. I was not bothered by the stress of the case or the Turcotte pressure, but I was plagued with thoughts of Ariana and the time we spent last night on Orbitus. Her business trip would end in the Whittemore Dome on Mars. As we talked last night at the Orbitus cafe's corner table, my tension had eased and I wondered why I had ever let her go. I sensed she had similar feelings when she suggested we meet at the Excelsior Hotel's restaurant in Livingston tomorrow night.

Chapter 3

I drifted between the edges of sleep and a full realization the man supposed to provide vital production information at this morning's breakfast lay dead, covered with icy blood in the desert. Mars's brown, crater-dotted soil, lifeless from a thousand kilometers out, was bright against dark space. I sat up as the Orbitus shuttle slowed amidst an assortment of beeps and a recliner sweep by the attendants. After traveling to the murder sight with Patenaude, my next move, if I stuck my nose into this mess, might involve a roverbus trip to Industrial Plant Five, and interviews with all plant personnel. I was, however, acutely aware of Desmond's fierce opposition to an evolving investigation. He would proceed only if he had control of the situation at the plant.

As the craft banked and fully rotated a hundred and eighty degrees for entry into the thin Martian atmosphere, many views were visible on the recliner window screen, but I had other things on my mind. Foremost was how Jason Rapp had any information at all about the goings on inside a plant thousands of kilometers away from his inner solar system stomping grounds. The shuttle fully faced the crisp yellow sun, reduced slightly in size from Orbitus, but noticeably smaller than the view from Earth. The tinted radiation shields darkened now and I shut my eyes. Rapp skipped breakfast, maybe an oversight, and headed directly to Mars, within kilometers of IP-5. In fact, on the way to the murder scene he had to pass or stop at IP-5, unless he took the long way around from Livingston via IP-7 and retreated along its connector road.

The craft shuddered at the atmospheric edges and my eyes remained closed. I didn't know Rapp personally, but his appearance at the black jack tables and sensitivity to losing the wad of droits, lent itself to another speculation, albeit unsubstantiated. His avoidance of the breakfast might reveal another plan; a plan to procure money. Obviously, he was aware the Turcottes were engaged in something nefarious at IP-5 or at least cognizant something was rotten in production. How Rapp came to know about that information was irrelevant right now, but blackmail could point toward his killer.

I pulled out my zip and pushed Patenaude's address. The transmission was scratchy through the atmosphere and he sounded as if he had a mouth full of his favorite dessert. "Jahn Patenaude."

"Are you eating the real cheesecake or the doctor recommended version?"

"The real thing. The hell with the doctors. Couldn't you wait another half an hour, Harry?"

"I can't get this thing off my mind. I need to talk to people at IP-5."

"Funny you should mention IP-5," said Patenaude, taking in more cheesecake. "The plant manager, Joe Lockheed."

"What about him?"

"Not around. Not at the plant. Not at his habitat connected to the IP-5 dome. Get this: Logs indicate Lockheed checked out a company rover at 12:47 PM."

"Rapp was killed an hour later, eight kilometers from the plant. Why would Lockheed leave the plant during a dust storm?"

"Good question, Harry," said Patenaude. "Strawberry cheesecake. Very good. Almost as good as cherry."

"You'd better watch your diet," I told him. "We need witnesses at the plant. Somebody who might have seen Rapp and Lockheed together."

The frequency wavered as the shuttle descended. "Well, Ed Stanton gave me the rover information and is supposed to get back to me, but he says the Turcottes, Brandon and Desmond are both out at IP-5."

"Something stinks and I don't like it."

Patenaude's signal went out. The brighter edges of the atmosphere separated a well-defined line against the outer space darkness. I clipped the zip on my belt and leaned back. Rapp was blackmailing Lockheed. What other explanation would fly against his quick departure from Orbitus? I wanted to know more about Rapp, but as we surged into the upper atmosphere, my anger toward Desmond Turcotte mounted like the pressure of an over-inflated dome on the planet's surface

* * * *

I saw the enveloping dust cloud from several thousand meters over the planet's surface. The charcoal tinted Livingston Dome rounded beautifully, bouncing sporadic bursts of reflected sunlight outward, but my eyes were drawn across the darkening rocky desert, blanketed by the sweeping gray storm. The digital overhead clock showed the shuttle was exactly on time as we swung over Livingston and prepared to bank for the port atop the dome.

I leaned against the portal's cold transparent silcoplast. Even IP-5 was hidden under the sand and wind. I rubbed my nose several times as I anguished about the source for Rapp's information. He needed someone to provide the IP-5 improprieties in order to pressure Lockheed. I knew I was forming an unavoidable list of facts into a theory dependent on my own prejudices and misconceptions. Underlying everything was the image of Rapp handing over the blue droit wad on Orbitus.

My shoulder pushed against the outer wall as we circled toward Livingston. The long gray runways crisscrossed the open area along the top of the dome. As we neared the upper area, the rest of the rounded enclosure below, vanished, and I had the sense as I always did, of landing on a flat planetary surface. I studied the pointed blue control towers and the hotels inside the clear silcoplast bubbles dotted like blisters on the top. The landing gear popped and we raced above grainy runway, finally making contact three seconds from four-thirty. Huge air lifters slowed the craft outside the port.

I was compelled to look back across the desert. The dark cloud lurked more ominous from here, but a surface tracer, captained by an experienced pilot, would very easily traverse even an ionized dust storm. I moved my leg rapidly up and down as we taxied back toward the port's transition surrounds.

I thought about my own people. Max and Jody were working on a minor customs case along the transport barriers outside lunar orbit. I smiled when I realized how the bionic Jody's rational personality forever grated on the suave Max's nerves, yet he somehow stayed working with her. Renie was another matter. I first met him when I arrested him five years ago for smuggling in the Hampshire Colony gutter districts. I saw cleverness and a sensitivity not even Renie knew he possessed. He could find anyone or anything and had the daring to pull it off. Somehow, Sadie kept all my people in line.

The surrounds diagonal doors revealed a hundred fingered locks as they slid open. An inner protective silcoplast transparency moved upward once the outer doors meshed back together. We soon rolled onto the port's inner runways. I yawned and tried to stop jiggling my leg, but Rapp's death gnawed at me like an incurable disease infecting my thoughts. I looked across the linear surface to the smooth tan hotel facade basking in a dim sunlight similar to arctic bases on earth. Patenaude was waiting somewhere inside the adjacent tower for an immediate departure via surface tracer, and perhaps, he now had additional information.

* * * *

I carried my containment bag down the ramp corridor into the crowded terminal. My gray haired, slightly overweight, friend spoke with several of his red uniformed security troopers. Patenaude never wore an official uniform. His blue succo fit his rounded body and the gold snaps were unbuttoned. The white neck liner bulged out of the succo. I scanned the terminal and checked the communication windows along the wall. I wanted to call Sadie and see what she had on Rapp.

Patenaude broke away from his men. "Harry, I'm glad you're here."

"Why, have you solved the Rapp murder?"

I remained deadpan, throwing off his concentration.

"Solved it? I don't even have the rover rental reports yet and Kranz is being difficult."

"Kranz is a pain … What about Rapp?" I asked as we headed for containment release and the rest of my bags.

"Ah … Spent two years in the detention wheel when he was nineteen and made his initial contacts with the Divone group."

I stopped and faced him. "Jahn, I spent my career chasing the Divone people. Frankly, they're too powerful and I don't want to waste my time."

"Rapp's been married four times. A real ladies man."

I started walking again. "Jahn, you're not listening."

"I am. Rapp's a gambler. He learned his trade in the detention wheel under the wing of the Divone people. Had a murder charge against him, but the Divone lawyers got him off because he worked in the Primo. A good place to pick up women."

"A real nice place the Primo." I stepped onto the mover and set my containment on the black, bubbled surface. "The Primo: Heartland of vulgarity and heathens … I miss it."

Patenaude smiled. "We should have rover reports before we board the tracer. My men can bring your containments to the Dillon."

"That's fine. I need to get to a window and call Sadie. How's Gwen?"

"With the kids and grand kids."

"I can't believe you're a grandfather. Makes me feel old." The mover dipped down toward the containment release. "This Rapp thing has a distinct Turcotte odor to it. Whatever happened over IP-5 must have been big."

"That investigation is not my concern right now." The mover leveled and I stepped onto the solid surface near the containment release. The clear transport tubes were empty and I headed toward the window kiosks.

"Where are you going Harry? We need to get to the tracer hanger."

"I'm calling Sadie."

"Okay." Patenaude whipped out his zip and shouted out orders about getting my containers to the Dillon.

I sat in front of the window and plugged in my zip. As containments shot through the clear overhead tubes and more passengers gathered around the deposit bins, my zip connected to my Orbitus office. Sadie sat at a keyboard in her bright blue succo. She smiled when she saw me. "Well, I see the shuttle made it in one piece and I still have a job."

I grinned "Oh?"

"I have an extensive report on Rapp. I was about to memo into your zip.

"He was a Divone man."

"Does the word scoundrel come to mind?" she asked.

"It does. Sadie, I'm trying to figure out how Rapp came into information about production problems in Turcotte Industrial Plant Five."

"I can have Renie track that down." I nodded and looked into her green eyes. "I think he's in the transaction locus."

"Not surprising. Listen, I'm about to leave on a tracer with Patenaude. We should be at the murder sight in about half an hour."

"Who are we working for in this one?" she asked.

"Purely curiosity at this point. I want to know why a guy who was supposed to meet me with information is now dead. The main focus is the Ed Stanton thing, which I guess will put me on the Turcotte payroll."

Patenaude took a seat behind the petition and activated the window.

"Harry, Max and Jody are wrapping up the Norris case. Can they reach you by zip later tonight your time?"

"Of course. I don't know if I'll have window access, but yes, have them call. I should have a better idea what my status is here and whether Ed Stanton wants me looking into any of this."

"Very well. You have a nice little trip into that dust."

"Just what I wanted," I said, trying to hear who Patenaude was talking on the window. "A journey across the dust of Mars. Thanks, Sadie."

I unclipped my zip and stood. Patenaude spoke to a man wearing a smooth green succo and a Livingston gate identification badge. The man explained something about rover rentals. I walked around the panel and Patenaude raised his finger as he spoke. "Yes, I understand, Mr. Forest, I have the list in my zip. What about times of rental?"

"Yup."

"And droit payment?" asked Patenaude.

"Yup."

"Can I call your people about any questions concerning these individuals?"

"Yup."

"Would they be on security windows?"

"What windows? We have privacy rights involved here."

"Thanks a lot," said Patenaude.

"Yup."

"He's a wealth of information."

Patenaude stood and tucked his zip in his succo. "I'm sick of hearing about privacy rights. We have a man dead in the desert."

"Privacy rights end when people get murdered," I said.

"Easier said than done. Listen, I have a memo from Stanton." I raised my brows and tilted my head. "Lockheed is definitely missing."

"The IP-5 plant manager." We headed toward the containment deposit bins. One of my containers sat cockeyed in the transparency. "Now, that is odd, Jahn. I wonder where he is."

Three of Patenaude's men appeared by the mover and headed toward the bins. "Do, you have a manifest number?"

I punched my zip. "Three-five-seven."

"Gentlemen, MN-357. Mr. Cobb is listed in the Hotel Dillon down in the dome."

"Yes, sir," said one of the young men.

"Come on, Harry," said Patenaude, picking up the pace toward the security elevator across the tubes. "Let's get up to the hanger and out to the murder sight."

*   *   *   *

I was surprised the flight was so rough. Fifteen years ago I was aboard a crashed tracer flight maybe six hundred kilometers away. One man was killed and rescue tracers didn't arrive for six hours. This present, ill-conceived flight into the dust storm now covering the Livingston Dome was worse. Two items Patenaude found on separate rover rental lists diverted my attention from the storm. A Turcotte employee named Jim Oakley drove his rover through LG-42 and onto the connector road to the Turcotte industrial plant managed by Lockheed. I thought we should check out Oakley's story and Patenaude agreed.

Patenaude's list showed a Samantha Evans rented a rover and departed through the same Livingston gate as Oakley. She had an attendant procure a rover at 10:16 a.m., nearly forty-five minutes after Oakley headed toward IP-5. The name Samantha Evans evoked memories of a possible bureau investigation or perhaps a long ago local security operation.

"That name sounds familiar," I told Patenaude. He imputed both names into his zip for background checks.

"Old girlfriend?" he asked.

I half-grinned as the pilot began a vertical descent. He looked back at Patenaude. "Inspector, we're docking at the portable dome set up by Lieutenant Kranz and his men. We won't be affected by the storm."

"It's by God's grace we're here at all," I said. The pilot nodded slowly. All of Patenaude's five security men had relief in their eyes. "Jahn, the name Samantha Evans relates to a some case I wasn't directly involved in. Could be five or six years ago. I remember reading reports. Something about a disappearance. Might have been on earth."

"You always remember every useless fact and case you ever heard of …" Patenaude stroked his chin. "Unless, the Turcottes invited Evans, why did she travel out to an industrial plant?"

"Another thing on our list of questions for Desmond Turcotte."

The tracer magnetically locked into the top of the portable dome. I was glad we were on the ground even though the sand grains pelted the tracer's outer shell. Two of Patenaude's men remotely slid the hatch and Kranz's grating voice shot through the ladder tunnel. I looked at Patenaude and shook my head.

"He's not that bad."

"The man likes to give orders because he sure as hell didn't like to follow orders when he was with the bureau."

"People do grow into their jobs, Harry."

Patenaude and I stood together as one of Kranz's men popped his head through the floor opening. "I trust you gentlemen enjoyed the ride."

"Ride, yes. Enjoy: no," I said.

"You must be Harry Cobb. The Lieutenant requests you get clearance from the Security Chief Burkhart before entering the dome."

"What kind of malarkey is that?"

"Lieutenant's orders, sir."

"Okay, maybe some people don't grow into their jobs," said Patenaude. He walked up to the opening and motioned the man back. Then he positioned himself on top of the stairs and maneuvered himself in a surprisingly agile manner into the tiny dome.

I crossed my arms and tried to remember more about Samantha Evans, but every time I tried to recount those days, memories of the arrogant Kranz ran rampart. I specifically recalled an incident on a lunar base where I directly told Kranz to search an abandoned warehouse and he brought his men in slowly, just to upset me. I put him on report and although I couldn't prove three contraband runners escaped through one of the basement locks, I blamed Kranz. The runners escape did not annoy me half as much as Kranz's obstreperous defiance.

Patenaude stuck his head up. "You may enter the royal castle now."

"What did you do, bribe him?" I asked and walked toward the ladder.

"Let's just say I know certain things about the good lieutenant." Patenaude had a twinkle in his blue eyes. "Come on, before they put the body in the containment bin."

A cocky smile broke across my face. "Was the dear boy being naughty?"

"You might say that," said Patenaude from below.

"Tell me more," I said and climbed onto the ladder.

"Then it wouldn't be a secret."

I moved my hands over the abrasive rungs as the air-cooled and the sand hit the thinner dome walls. Hebon towers shined white blocks of light across a rusty, sand laden, half buried rover. The bubble top was pierced open as if someone had cut through the silcoplast with a thin blade and the tire treads were mostly buried in the sand. Red glowing coils from Kranz's field heaters pushed a semblance of warmth into the dome, but the air was still cold enough to see your breath. An air purifier hummed behind Rapp's rover near the locks connecting Kranz's security tracer.

Three security men with velvet blue outer coats hovered around a dark containment bin. Kranz, in a maroon realball cap and the bureau's red military fatigues, sat on scaffolding above the rover. When he saw me he smiled. "Commander Cobb. We meet again."

"You're out of uniform, Kranz."

"You're lucky I let you in here."

I looked over at Patenaude by the rover. He rolled his eyes and then peered inside. "Oh, I don't know how much luck had to do with it."

Kranz thought about that for a while and then yelled at the men near the containment bin. "Get the body out."

"Wait," said Patenaude. "Harry, take a look at this."

I glanced at Kranz, huffing under his breath, and then I studied the melted silcoplast on Rapp's rover. Only a pinpoint pulser would so cleanly slice the silcoplast. When I rounded the bin I saw Jason Rapp's contorted face. "Looks, like he was gasping for air."

"Dead is dead, Cobb," said Kranz.

I didn't acknowledge him, but instead looked at the dried blood on Rapp's blue fatigues. His head was dipped on his shoulder and his once neat brown hair was matted on his head. "Do we have pulser fire angles and intensity?"

"The preliminary investigation is complete, compadre. Let's put him in the bin and get the hell back to Livingston."

"Where is Stanton?" I asked.

"Who cares?" replied Kranz. "Get the body out."

"No wait. What's the damned rush?" I asked and now stared at Kranz. "We just got here."

"And we're all hungry and tired. We've been out here for three hours."

"Even dogs have to be fed," I whispered to Patenaude.

"Any other pinpoint murders around Livingston recently?"

"Save your babbling for the courtroom. Nobody hired you anyway."

"Harry is here on my authority," said Patenaude and he stepped back from the rover opening. "Ya, as a matter of fact. The end of June. One of the tram operators between domes. Guy named Burroughs. We can look into it when we get back. Check pulser frequencies."

"Ya, you do that," said Kranz, jumping down from the scaffolding. "Time to fold up tent. You saw the body-he's dead. What do you say, Inspector?"

Patenaude winked and I nodded. "I would suggest you go back into your tracer, Lieutenant, and munch on the food provisions."

Kranz crunched his teeth and motioned his men back through the little dome's bottom lock. I watched him disappear inside the other tracer and then I peered into Patenaude's crisp blue eyes. "If I were a man of revenge I'd send that son of a bitch on permanent patrol in the Transaction Zone."

"He'll be right at home," said Patenaude, pulling out his zip.

As I stared at Rapp's smooth hands, Patenaude called his office back in Livingston. I pieced Rapp's disjointed life together with the limited information Sadie and Patenaude had given me. Lockheed was missing, but until I could place him on this connector road around quarter of two this afternoon, I discounted him as involved in the murder. It was more than coincidence. Rapp had ventured to the facility with knowledge of that plant's problems and cover up. How he came into such information might prove critical as to why he was killed.

"I have the manufacturer of the pinpoint that killed Burroughs," said Patenaude, breaking my concentration. "A facility in a commerce colony midway between earth and us. Manufactured 2134 and sold to a man named Cauldwell, residence in numerous places."

"Who the hell is he?" I asked.

"We're checking. One of my investigators, Tom Doherty says not many people went out Livingston's south gates with the storm brewing. He's concerned about this guy Oakley who did arrive at IP-5 around quarter past twelve and, according to the foreman, Orby, he left a half an hour later on the IP-7 connector road. Same as Rapp, but—"

"Oakley was on the same road as Rapp?"

"So was Lockheed, my friend. He left from a different IP-5 lock. Orby was talking with Tommy Doherty when Desmond Turcotte himself cut off the conversation."

"Orby's testimony is critical, Jahn. We need legal action on this."

"I know. It means breaking the Turcotte hold on the court magistrates."

I told Patenaude I still had connections in the bureau and would use them against the Turcottes if necessary to procure Orby's testimony. I scanned the rocks and sand around rover as the storm pummeled the portable dome. "Has anyone surveyed the sand here? We haven't even read Kranz's report. I'd also like soil samples to compare the magnetic alignment to both Lockheed's and Oakley's rovers."

"Wherever the hell those rovers are," said Patenaude, motioning to one of his men. He sent the kid into the lock to get Kranz's report.

"And Samantha Evans."

"Doherty has her vehicle impounded," said Patenaude.

"Really?"

Patenaude turned toward the lock as his man returned into the dome. "What's the problem?"

"He has the report in his zip and he's transmitted a copy to the security port."

I pressed my lips together and felt the frustration mounting. Patenaude held my arm briefly as I left the rover and marched past the kid into the connector lock. Kranz sat, gnawing on ship's provisions, in the command recliner, and his feet were propped on the forward console. He laughed when he saw me and threw a palm size disk in my direction. "You're a pain in the ass, Cobb."

I bent over and held the disk in my hand. As much as I wanted to knock my fist into his jaw, I moved into the lock. I could hear him mutter something back in the tracer. I gave the disk to Patenaude and we studied the reading on one of the enlarged security zips. Most everything was in order, which annoyed me, but no soil samples were taken. We filled a few containers and I gazed back toward Kranz's lock.

"Let's get out of here, Jahn."

"What about Kranz?"

I shook my head. "Let's go."

CHAPTER 4

The meal at the Excelsior erased the emotional onslaught of the day's investigation. I sat with Patenaude and a few of his officers at a huge round table next to a six-foot square zip window. Gwen Patenaude, her white hair cut short, stood in their habitat with Patenaude's daughter, son-in-law, and three young grand children, darting like errant meteorites across the room.

I lifted a second stein of Amber Chill, a high potency beer from a well-known lunar company. "And Jahn, of course, watches the children."

Gwen laughed. "Just like when the kids were growing up. He arrives home and is the hero."

"You wouldn't catch me hanging out around the house. I'd rather be under pulser fire in the Transaction Zone." Patenaude moved a white silcoplast fork through the large ripe strawberries and scooped up a syrup-covered chunk of smooth yellow cheesecake. "It's safer!"

"What about you, Harry?" asked Gwen. "You stayed devoted to your career and never married."

"Sometimes fate has a life of its own," I said, wondering if I was too profound. "I do have a lot of nieces and nephews."

"Here on Mars?"

"Earth. My family is mostly on earth. Los Angeles and northern California."

"Jahn and I had a wonderful trip down the California coast five years ago."

Patenaude gulped his jafrin from a magenta mug. "Try nine years ago, Gweny."

"Time flies," she said.

A red memo flashed in the window's lower right corner.

"We have a memo," said Patenaude. "I'll be back in less than an hour, sweetheart."

"I've heard that before," said Gwen as one of the kids jumped into her lap.

"Bye, granddad," said the little girl.

"Good-bye, Jenny. Bye Matt. Bye Karen."

The window closed into a small dot and quickly reopened to a playback of the thin Doherty in his blue fatigues. A dusty rover was parked in a security lab. The lower digit clock noted the report was made ten minutes ago. "Jahn, Samantha Evans' rover is behind me. A couple of things. This rover's dust aligns magnetically with the particles you brought back."

"Thank you, Harry," said Patenaude.

I shrugged my shoulders as Doherty's memo continued.

"This rover was rented at ten sixteen this morning by a woman—five foot seven, blonde hair, and blue eyes. I have conflicting reports here. Her credit listing puts her on Banfield Lunar Colony in a small habitat. According to calls I placed to neighbors, Evans is away all the time. Habitat was purchased six years ago.

But I have an additional report from earth. Baltimore."

"That was it!" I said. "A pinpoint attack and the woman disappeared. I'm sure it was Samantha Evans."

"A pinpoint attack and the woman disappeared," said Doherty. Patenaude smiled. "Some rumors suggest she faked a pinpoint attack. More than likely I think she just disappeared. This woman also had a criminal background, including arrests for fraud and grand larceny. That's it from here, Jahn. We'll go over the rover again tomorrow. Oh, I called Oakley's habitat like you wanted. His wife reports he's not around. Never around. She had already called the local security port. I'll talk to you."

"Well, well," said Patenaude. "Our little Miss Evans has a past."

I pinched my chin. Doherty's report left me unnerved.

"Rapp was from Baltimore, Jahn."

"Oh, boy," said Patenaude. He finished the jafrin and looked across the restaurant.

"Jafrin will keep you awake."

"I may need to stay awake."

I turned as Desmond Turcotte, his black hair brushed back perfectly, marched ahead of his shorter brother into the restaurant. Even at this late hour Desmond wore a red succo with gold buttons and a gold neck liner. His dark eyes focused on Pate-naude. "I see the good inspector has ample free time on his schedule."

Patenaude stood, but I remained seated. I still remembered Desmond as a smart-mouthed little brat running around Jarred Turcotte's office twenty years ago. Patenaude quickly shook Desmond's hand. "Why are you here, Desmond?"

"Why am I here?" he asked and smiled at his brother.

"Brandon, he hasn't used his brilliant powers of deduction to understand my concerns."

"Seems as though you have *ample* concerns," I said loudly.

Desmond quickly turned toward me. He raised his left brow and nearly smiled. "I thought you were in retirement."

"Technically, I am on your payroll."

Brandon's brow creased, but Desmond was unfettered.

"A call from Ed Stanton does not warrant any association with the Turcotte name. Only I will deem who is and is not on the Turcotte payroll."

I stood and walked by Patenaude. Desmond didn't flinch when I moved within centimeters of his taller frame. "Does your father have a working knowledge of the operations of Industrial Plant Five?"

"Father has a more intra-solar system role nowadays," said Desmond, his voice shifting from confrontational to charming.

"My father, always admired your bureau record, Harry. Please consider yourself always a friend of the Turcottes."

"That is reassuring. Where is your father now?"

"In the Caribbean," said Brandon.

"Oh," I said, raising my brows, but I soon found Desmond's arm around my shoulder. He walked me a few feet from the table.

"Jarred is fully aware of certain production problems in IP-5. Things that have been changed and are not important now."

I looked at his hand, still on my arm. He released his grip.

"You think Jason Rapp thought those problems were important?"

"Rapp is dead and on my property. My chief engineer in IP-5 is missing. I want you to find the truth."

I stared at him for a few moments. "Do you?"

"Why, yes, of course."

"Desmond, I don't trust you."

He tilted his chin up and laughed. "That's why I always liked you. You speak your mind and you're so cynical. I can assure you I want my IP-5 engineer cleared."

"Oh? Where is he?"

"Finding him is a priority."

"My guess is he's hiding out with or without your help in one of your facilities. IP-5 or IP-7."

"Then, can I credit you a thirty droit retainer?"

"I want a fifty droit retainer with expenses," I said and tried to second guess how much he really wanted me in the investigation.

"Okay."

"And tell me what was going on at IP-5."

"I shant go that far. Ed wanted you to look at the overall picture. But with specifics, we're talking about trade secrets."

"Desmond, you risk not having my services."

"No mind …"

"I'll follow this up under certain conditions. You let me have full run of your facilities here on Mars. I want to speak with Ed Stanton and all personnel. And I want Patenaude with me."

"Agreed."

"And don't be holding back anything or I'm off the case."

Desmond produced his overbearing, fixed smile. "I wouldn't think of putting the investigation in jeopardy."

"Oh, yes, you would."

I walked by him and he uttered something about not bothering to call his father. Brandon was enjoying a stein of Amber Chill and talking with Patenaude about a realball game he went to last night. Patenaude looked at Desmond, now at the bar, and then at me. "What's the good news?"

"I'm officially working for the Turcottes on this."

"Really?"

"Great," said Brandon, shaking my hand with a grip stronger than Desmond's feeble grasp. "My father always speaks well of you."

I thought about asking Brandon about IP-5, but figured Desmond had already browbeaten him into silence. "I look forward to your father's return."

"Desmond gave him and my mother an extensive trip."

"I bet he did." I was beginning to question whether Jarred knew about IP-5 or if he did maybe he was letting Desmond handle it. "Brandon, did you know Jason Rapp?"

Brandon shook his head and sipped some more chill. He made eye contact and I believed he was telling the truth. "No, but I'm not sure about Joe Lockheed."

"Neither am I." I was more convinced as Desmond cantered back across the restaurant, whatever improprieties occurring at IP-5, as illegal or nefarious as they might seem, were far less important than Rapp's possible blackmail of Lockheed. "What kind of a man was Lockheed?"

"Joe Lockheed," said Desmond upon his return. "Was a no-nonsense man who did his job well."

"No-nonsense meaning he wouldn't take any guff from anybody?" I asked.

"No … the man did his job."

"He lived his job," said Brandon.

"My brother is correct. You could always rely on Joe."

I sat down at the table again and thought about the cocky Rapp.

"Listen, Desmond. I know you can't tell me the inner workings of your plant, but what if Rapp knew what you knew."

"Blackmail, the oldest game around." He gazed toward a taller woman with long brown hair back at the entrance. "Almost the oldest game. That's a great theory, Harry, except Joe did nothing to be blackmailed about."

"No, *he* didn't."

"I will overlook that remark. We have to be going," he said, looking at the brunette again. "Come on, Brandon."

"Nice chatting with you," said Brandon, leaving the stein on the table.

Everyone exchanged handshakes. Desmond and Brandon parted company. Desmond rendezvoused ahead and slipped his arm around a woman by the bar. I turned to Patenaude. "I think Ed wanted answers that Desmond wouldn't give him. But I tell you: I want to know what the hell is going on out at IP-5."

"So, do I, but he's not going to tell us."

"Damned Turcotte power. It might take months to get the trade boards to look into it. Desmond would block it all the way."

"Hence, the arrogance," said Patenaude.

"I'm contacting Jarred Turcotte."

"Good luck. I'm sure Desmond somehow controls access to his father, too. Very clever how he moved Jarred into space. Jarred handles expanding the Turcotte holdings, giving Desmond full reign here."

My mind drifted. I daydreamed about being with Ariana tomorrow evening. Old memories of the towering Gondola falls, cascading off the sunlit jagged mountain cliffs materialized in my head. Ten years ago I had flown in from an investigation on earth and met her at a Mars social gathering. From the first moment we were attracted to each other. We stayed out all night and she booked the time in the dome. I was tired from months of continuous work and Barsoom's mystery was just what we both needed.

I let my mind wander back to the mountaintop chateau overlooking the rope bridge that bowed over the canyon. Ariana wore only a velvet red succo as we walked up the stones to the chateau. My thoughts were shattered when Patenaude touched my wrist.

"Sorry, Jahn," I said with a smile. "I'm having dinner tomorrow night with Ariana."

Patenaude raised his bushy brows. "Well, well, I see old fires can be rekindled."

"I am afraid you might be right."

"She is a powerful woman now that Cervantes is dead. Amalgamated Sureties is no small potato. Well, before the evening fireworks, kindly meet me in my office tomorrow morning. I want to get this case over el pronto. I don't like bucking the Turcottes. I want the murderer in custody and then go back to my run of the mill cases."

"What time?" I asked.

"Meet me at eight-thirty. Maybe we can get out to IP-5 and interview Orby."

"Tomorrow?"

"Don't worry, I'll have you back in Livingston before evening. I just hope you know what you're doing, Harry."

"So do I, Jahn. So, do I."

CHAPTER 5

Jason Rapp's corpse, aligned on a forensic scanning table inside the Hasbrook Dome, was eerie on Patenaude's office window. Without touching a pulser beam to his body, technicians mapped Rapp's internal organs. For the past two hours tissues, organs, and systems were magnified and extrapolated with graphs and data. Rapp's liver was not in the best of shape, but his heart was strong and not touched by the pinpoint beam. His lungs were punctured and sliced in several areas as the killer dragged the beam downward. The damage was not enough to kill him, but made him gurgle for breath and drown in his own blood. Insignificant abrasions, probably occurring when the beam retracted, appeared on his shoulder and arm.

I winced as the forensics lecture continued on the window. "I don't think I need to know the man had a bout with the flu when he was fourteen."

"Don't you like details, Harry?" asked Patenaude.

"I like details just fine when they have relevance." I walked over to the water containment and poured myself a cup of cool water.

"You want some jafrin?" asked Patenaude.

"As a matter of fact, maybe I do." I drank the water anyway as Patenaude moved into the main office. Ten minutes ago he procured a playback of the rental manager. Under threat of a magistrate order, the guy described a tall blonde with blue eyes. It's on the security scan. He wasn't sure about a ten year old image of Samantha Evans that Patenaude had found on an old media disk.

I called out when he neared the food alcove. "You know this case is starting to get on my nerves."

"I never would have guessed."

"Don't we have any more recent images of Evans?"

"Harry, she's been missing for six years."

"Somebody's pretending to be her."

"You don't know that."

I took another swig of water and let it stay in my mouth, chilling my teeth until it warmed to body temperature. I walked back to the window, grabbed the controller and reversed the playback. From the doorway Patenaude held two steaming cups of jafrin. I turned toward the array of buttons under the little screen mirroring the forward window. "This thing is really annoying me."

"What's the matter didn't you sleep last night?"

"As a matter of fact," I said, taking the jafrin mug. I sniffed the mint-flavored batch. "For the record, I didn't sleep at all."

Patenaude, smiled, raised his brows and took the controller from my hand. "Where do you want to be on the playback?"

I brought the warm mixture to my lips and allowed the soothing blend to trickle down my throat. The effect, as usual, was instant, easing my sinus headache, and sharpening my alertness. "I want to see the angle of fire and speculation on the shooter."

"Forty-three, sixteen. Ballistics section, go."

"Forty-three, sixteen. How am I supposed to know that?" I asked and took in some more jafrin. "Go … you make it sound like your asking your dog to fetch the evening paper." The disk stopped at a depiction of the rover, a simulated killer in a silver terrain suit and red beams in a series of frames, showing the exact angle of fire. "The problem with these simulations is they look so real."

"We've come a long way," said Patenaude, taking his seat.

"Ya, but we run the risk of believing the damned thing because it seems too real. Look at that window. It's like we're there yesterday afternoon. Power of the pinpoint was sixty-five pulses per second. Okay, I'll buy that."

"I'm glad," said Patenaude, sampling the jafrin. He smacked his lips. "You are in a bad mood."

I didn't argue the point as I approached the window. "You want to know what bothers me?"

"Okay, Harry, what bothers you?"

"Angle of fire was only slightly higher than horizontal to Rapp."

"Why does that bother you?" he asked, and looked amused at my crotchety attitude.

"No, that isn't what bothers me. Beam was 1.89 centimeters, but they automatically tell us the killer was 1.82 meters. That's ludicrous."

"Why? That the angle somebody that height would—"

"Did anyone bother to tell that smart-ass machine that we were in the middle of a dust storm? You saw the sands. They shifted every few minutes with the fury."

"Good point."

"Which means height and angle are useless. What about this pinpoint?"

Patenaude set his jafrin mug on the table. I gulped my own jafrin as he called somebody in his office on the zip and requested an update on the manufacture and identity of the pulser. I realized how much I had rounded off the pulse and size of the beam when he repeated the exact measurements down to the last decimal point, critical pieces of data for tracing a weapon. "I understand."

"What happened?"

"They will have it on the window momentarily." I sat down and rubbed my eyes. "It's not the case that's got you all fired up."

"What do you mean?" I asked, my eyes closed as I pinched the bridge of my nose.

"You're scared to death you might get involved with Ariana again."

My eyes opened slowly like the transition surrounds on a land dome and Patenaude's wide smile came into focus. "You think you know me so well."

"I do."

"Sure, I'm asking myself why I bothered to cross the gaming floor."

"I think you'll have to let it play out, my friend."

"You may be right." I squinted as studied the pinpoint data filling the window's lower corner in bright red letters.

Manufacturer: Elton Ballistics
Commerce Plant Alpha
date of manufacture: 11–22–37
shipped to Best Sales, earth warehouse
Baltimore, Maryland, USA 5–29–39
purchase information:

J.W. Cauldwell
16 Brubacker Drive
Norton, MD
permit: # 678906
b. 4–28–2092
d.10–11–2139

"*Cauldwell*? What the hell is going on here?" I finished the jafrin, plugged my zip into the side window, and signaled Max. "Are you thinking what I'm thinking, Jahn?"

"You mean that Burroughs was from Baltimore and so was Samantha Evans and he was killed by Cauldwell's pinpoint."

"That's exactly what I'm thinking."

Max was dressed in a textured banal fabric blue succo with a ruffled neck liner and his dark hair trimmed symmetrically down to the centimeter. I had never seen his appearance compromised. His voice reflected his Noville education background.

"Harry, I was about to memo your zip. How are you this morning?"

"Lousy, how are you?"

"I'm fine and eager to help you on this case involving Jason Rapp. We are on the Rapp case, right?"

"I guess we are. Who knows at this point?" Jody, her brown hair cut short, was dressed in a one-piece olive jumper.

"Jody …"

"What?" she answered in her bionic monotone.

"How are you?"

"Is that a rhetorical question?" she asked.

"No, just a greeting."

"Oh, yes … Hello and hello, Inspector Patenaude."

Max leaned to the left. "Oh, I do apologize, Inspector for the oversight. Good to see you again."

"Good to see you, Max."

"What have you got?" I asked as Patenaude pointed at his mug, but the jafrin had sufficiently awakened me. I shook my head. "Samantha Evans' body was never found, yet she is here on Mars, in a rental rover garage, using current credit."

"May I?" asked Jody, stepping in front of Max.

"Manners are not something I expect," said Max and he motioned her center scanner.

"Background checks indicate Samantha Evans was J. W. Cauldwell's lover. And Cauldwell's pulser killed Burroughs."

"Max, Cauldwell's pulser killed Jason Rapp!" I exclaimed.

"Interesting …"

"Cauldwell was at his main residence in Platinum City when, Evans disappeared on a trip to Platinum City. A report was filed 10–7–39 by local security."

"And she disappeared just before Cauldwell's death." I looked at Patenaude. He leaned toward the window. "But Cauldwell's weapon killed Burroughs, long after he was dead. I'm telling you Evans' disappearance was no accident. Jody, did Evans really pay for the rover rental?"

"An attendant rented it with her approval on her credit and brought the rover to the rim road around Livingston. The images from the scan, taken from the side, look like her. But who knows? Even the enhancements are bad."

"Was there a palm scan or genetic scan."

"Harry," said Max. "You know as well as I most merchants are just interested in payment."

I nodded and closed my eyes briefly. "What else?"

"Cauldwell died of a heart malfunction at his home in Platinum City, October 11, 2139. I am currently awaiting forensic and biographical data on Mr. Cauldwell. Additional information about the Cauldwell-Evans relationship would prove useful. I am having problems checking Evans' credit."

"Call Renie. He knows people who can find out that information."

"Of course, Renie's associates are … varied."

"Well put. Listen, Jahn and I are checking out Lockheed and Oakley. Both men are still missing. We're traveling out to IP-5 this morning, but I am now considering missing Samantha Evans as the third suspect."

"Yes, that is a given. You mean the Turcottes are cooperating?" asked Max.

"Cooperating? Desmond is paying me a retainer and expenses."

"Unheard of."

"Mr. Turcotte has sufficient funds," said Jody without moving a facial muscle.

"Forgive my friend, Inspector. She takes things very literally, which sometimes works to my advantage."

"Max, let's make it a point to check in this evening." Patenaude smiled but did not look at me. "Early this evening. I'll call you."

"Understood. Good luck at IP-5, Harry … Inspector."

"Nice chatting with you both."

"Thanks for your help, Jody," I said and awaited her reply.

"That is within my job description."

Max rolled his eyes. "Come with me, Jody. We have work to do. Good day, gentlemen."

The window closed and I pointed at Patenaude. "You knew I was thinking about my dinner with Ariana when I said I was calling Max."

"Who me?"

I tried not to grin as I stood. "Well?"

"Well, what?"
"Are we going to IP-5?"
"That is within my job description."

Chapter 6

Under clear, pale green sky, hundreds of tapering brown sand mounds covered the connector road to IP-5. Large, slow moving yellow cleaner trucks hummed, sucked up the material into a surround cover and then shot the sand out a side chute into the cold, rock strewn desert. I stared at Patenaude, sitting across from me on the rover bench. "This is your fault."

"I thought a ride through the desert my improve your disposition."

"Are you saying I'm moody this morning?" I smiled and walked up to the roverbus driver. The cleaner truck finally cleared the embankment and we pulled around. IP-5's translucent white dome and several connector tubes and smaller domes spread out below the next angled ridge. "Good, it's about time. If we went by tracer, we'd be having lunch by now."

"If Desmond would spring for it," said Patenaude.

The machine's vacuum and rotor was louder as we passed and headed toward the open plant road. I panned the rolling valley, dotted with craters of varying sizes, toward IP-7. Eight kilometers away Jason Rapp was murdered yesterday in his rented rover. Samantha Evans baffled me. Renie would uncover credit information and Patenaude had an alert memo tagging any future Evans credit usage. I returned to the bench.

Patenaude crossed his legs. "Don't worry, Harry. I have a feeling things will improve for you as the day wears on."

I smiled and stared out the side window. The roverbus moved onto a dark, paved area, still sprinkled brown with dust, and bordering one of the side domes. The smooth gray garage door moved upward as we approached and drove into the transition surrounds. I picked up my office containment and shuffled to the front of the vehicle. The dim light surrounded us as the door rumbled back in place and air pushed across the pad from side vents.

When the pressure stabilized the driver moved the roverbus through a narrow corridor linking to a brighter area inside the main dome. White hebon bulbs highlighted gray steel bars, stacked in prodigious bins a hundred meters up the grainy white dome. I saw little Ed Stanton, his gray hair bursting under the rim of his red hard hat. He crossed the concrete with yellow suited plant personnel. Green transport trucks with tires the size of my Orbitus habitat, shifted mammoth shiny steel beams toward pressurized cranes positioned near the stacks.

"Which one is Orby?" I asked Patenaude as he joined me up front.

"Guy in back of Ed Stanton with the green hard hat. Skull traced hair cut."

"I see him." Orby had a fat face and wide shoulders. "He looks like a foreman. I want to know where the hell Joe Lockheed is."

"We'll hear what they have to say."

The roverbus door opened. I thanked the driver for a safe trip, but cautioned I was inclined to board a tracer for the return trip to Livingston. I stepped down the metal stairs and onto the concrete. Ed Stanton shook my hand. "I understand your officially hired, Harry."

"So, Desmond says."

Stanton shook hands with Patenaude and introduced the men from the plant. We were given red hard hats and directed across the concrete to an exterior elevator parked at the base of a towering gray wall. At the top was a long row of clear silcoplast.

"What about Lockheed?" I asked as we traversed the plant.

"He's still missing," said Stanton. "But we have some pertinent information."

"Oh?"

"Yes, security playbacks show Joe left here at 12:47 . He took the connector road to IP-7."

"How do you know that?" asked Patenaude.

"We'll show you the disk. 2:12 PM he arrived at IP-7."

I stopped and they all turned. "You can't tell me Desmond didn't know this yesterday."

"You can ask him, he's up top."

"I will," I said and we again headed toward the elevator.

"What we found on the playback and interviews with Bud Kearny, Joe's counterpart at IP-7 was interesting." Orby pushed a button and the door opened. We filed inside and Stanton continued. "Joe's t-suit was covered with dust."

"Then he must have stepped out of his rover," said Patenaude.

"Correct. And there's more."

We slowly rose above the voluminous stacking area." But he really is missing," I said.

"Yes, we have a playback from last night showing Joe stuffing the dusty suit into a zap duct. That evidence is gone now, but we do have Bud's report and the rover itself. Tests indicate Joe was in the dust storm."

"We know that, Ed," I said and we came to a stop near the top steel stacks. "I want to know where he went after he zapped the suit."

Stanton turned as Orby opened the door. A slew of offices light with more fleshy hebons were visible behind the lobby and reception desk. We strutted past several tall, green plants and Stanton raised his finger. "Don't be so quick to accuse Joe, Harry. Orby has a very interesting account of yesterday's activities here at the plant. We'll speak in my office."

I was escorted with the others to a set of blue doors marked, **SECURITY,** at the end of the corridor. Stanton flicked a controller, punched in a code, and the doors parted. A semi-circular desktop was blanketed with the fiery orange glow from the smelting ovens below. The huge vats, heated by brilliant red linear tubes, constantly dipped silver-blue liquid steel into the long, dark molding trays. I leaned against the silcoplast berm and saw men in green suits with bubble protectors work the upper region while others followed the process on windows above. The steel bars chugged along a conveyer belt and were gradually cooled behind black, vertical slats. I remembered Desmond and Jarred brought me through that area a few years back. Now I wondered what went wrong down there and how Rapp found out about it.

Stanton closed the outer doors and the hebons brightened. He motioned to Orby at the other end of the table. "Okay, Bill, brief them."

Everyone placed their zips on the table in unison and I smiled at Patenaude. Orby stared though the silcoplast at the inner plant, tightened his brow and squinted as he turned. "Yesterday during the twelve o'clock lunch shift, I heard some commotion down in the plant itself."

"The manufacturing portion?" asked Patenaude.

"Yes, sir." I was certain Desmond had rehearsed Orby's account. "I observed from the upper walkway an argument between Mr. Jason Rapp and Joe Lockheed."

"Arguments can be both subjective and at different levels of intensity," I said.

"It was a violent argument. Mr. Rapp continuously followed Joe Lockheed down the cooling lane. You can't see the lane from here, but I would be glad to bring you down there for all that it matters. Joe kept shaking his head and yelling that he had enough."

"Enough of what?" asked Patenaude.

Stanton pushed his controller and the words **SOUND PLAYBACK** appeared on the center window screen. "Enough of being blackmailed."

"That's no surprise," I said and Orby started the amplified playback.

"… you are. You're a low life that … every time you come to Mars looking for money. It … the fourth time I … had it! I have had it!"

"… your set. I have the ability to … of the right people. You and the Turcottes would be ruined. Don't you … of what I need."

"No, I won't do it any more. I have had enough! Get out! Get out or—"

I looked at Stanton. "Or what?"

"That's all we have."

Patenaude rolled his eyes. "I would like that playback analyzed."

"You'd have to clear that with Desmond.

"The hell with Desmond. I'll get a court order!" said Pate-naude. He banged his fist on the table.

The center table window brightened with Desmond's image. "There will be no court order, Inspector. It isn't necessary."

"You're right, Desmond, "I said. "Since you have been listening to this conversation and the sound, I would assume you realize that Joe Lockheed's next sentence threatened Rapp with death."

"I know nothing of the sort. I think Bill Orby should finish this story."

"Your story," I said.

"I would advise you, Harry, you are on retainer for me. I am just trying to help you."

"You mean divert."

"No mind … My, my you've become so cynical since your bureau days. Do continue your account, Bill, for Mr. Cobb and the Inspector."

Orby's face tensed. He cleared his throat. "Jim Oakley usually works weekends. He chose to enter the plant yesterday and proceed up to the lunchroom, but with something he retrieved from his locker."

"This sure as hell sounds like a set-up," said Patenaude.

"Think again, Inspector," said Desmond, his image in a corner box. I saw a playback of the lanky, sandy haired Oakley, a man in his thirties, reach behind the locked door. He stepped forward, looked around, and tucked something in his coat pocket.

"There it is. A pinpoint."

"You don't know that either," I said.

"Oh, yes we do," said Desmond as the playback advanced and then froze. A magnified image of Oakley's pocket showed a pinpoint pulser's silver grooved handle. "What do you think now?"

"Like Jahn said, We'd like to verify the disk," I said and Desmond laughed. "I'm serious. How do I know this isn't an attempt to cover for Joe Lockheed?"

"Perhaps you need more evidence."

"Please." I turned to Patenaude. "Where is Oakley, Jahn?"

"Missing."

An exterior window scanner showed a rover bouncing down the connector road from IP-5 toward the dark dust clouds and IP-7. "You can check the side tag if you wish. Ed already has. This is Rapp leaving for IP-7."

"Why?" I asked.

Stanton walked around the table and faced me. "Harry, Joe told Rapp he was leaving for a prior appointment at IP-7. We have that playback also."

"So, you're saying Rapp left to follow Lockheed?" asked Patenaude.

"No, he left five minutes before Joe Lockheed," said Stan-ton. "Joe threatened to go to the Turcottes and the authorities about the blackmail."

"I suppose you have that conversation, too," I said to Desmond on the window.

"We do," answered Desmond.

"Did Rapp specifically say he was going to kill Lockheed? He may have wanted to continue the argument at IP-7."

Desmond grinned and shook his head. "Things get complicated. We all know the position of Rapp's rover between the ridges next to the crater gorge. I think he waited in the lurch for Lockheed."

"You don't know that," I said and leaned toward Desmond's image. "Do you have playbacks of anything on the connector road?"

"We have nothing on the road," said Stanton. "But we do have Jim Oakley following both men onto the connector road."

I exhaled and sat down. For second I closed my eyes. Then I propped my elbows on the table and set my chin on my knuckles as I thought about Oakley's motives. "Why would Oakley give a damn about any of this? And why did he take a pinpoint from his locker? On the far side of the room Patenaude called his office on the zip. "Was he trying to kill Lockheed or Rapp?"

"I told you it got complicated," said Desmond with a smirk, making my blood race faster. "I think it is incumbent on you gentlemen to find out that information"

"Where is Lockheed, Desmond? Are you hiding him?"

"Don't be absurd."

I pointed toward the silcoplast. "And what happened down there in the plant that allowed Rapp to blackmail Joe Lockheed?"

"That is confidential company information."

Now the anger surged in my gut and I stood. "Then you get yourself another boy. I'm off this."

"Now, now, now … I would ask you to reconsider, Harry."

"And get suckered in to your cover-up? Forget it," I said, looking at Patenaude, still on the zip. "I'm heading back to Livingston and stay the night, and then I'm going back to Orbitus. You people worry about your shenanigans down here, I'm heading home."

I took two steps toward Patenaude. He raised his finger and turned as he continued on the zip. I pressed my lips, pushed the window pad and Desmond's image disappeared. "Come on Jahn, let's go."

Patenaude tucked his zip into his pocket and nodded. The intensity of his blue eyes told me he had new information. I said nothing and neither did he. I shook hands with Stanton. He offered to bring us back to the transition surrounds. I quickly squelched that idea and Patenaude and I exited the room.

"Harry, you shouldn't have quit the case."

"The Turcottes are too powerful for their own good. I don't care what Desmond wants. I don't care who killed Rapp. I'm going to have dinner with Ariana and let the chips fall where they may."

Patenaude followed me into the elevator. The doors opened and he typed something into his zip as we sunk slowly to ground level.

Rapp was tapping Oakley's wife

"Come on …" I shouted, knowing we probably monitored.

"What a soap opera."

"It's true."

"Great."

The scenario fell into place like hebons gradually illuminating a darkened room. Oakley was an employee right here in IP-5 and had access to the plant production. He knew what happened up here and must have told his wife. Rapp somehow pirated the information from the wife. Although speculating, I knew I was right.

* * * *

"Do you still want to get off the case?" asked Patenaude as the roverbus rocked along the connector road to Livingston. I clamped my jaw and stared across the rolling rock plains. I had said nothing about the case since we left the IP-5 surround.

"You have two people with motives and opportunity."

"Three," I said.

"I knew you couldn't stop thinking about this."

"I'm not in the habit of working for nothing, Jahn."

"We'll add you on the force as a consultant."

I turned back and looked him in the eye. "What makes you think you could afford my fees?"

"Knowing your altruistic nature."

"Altruism yes. Working for nothing, no." I looked outside the roverbus again.

"Samantha Evans rented a rover, now covered with dust configured to the murder scene dust, and she was a playing around with the original owner of the pinpoint that killed Rapp."

I closed my eyes. Rapp's return to the surface of Mars found its nexus out in the desert, a perfect isolated area for three individuals track him down. I focused on Patenaude when I opened my eyes. "You know what's bothering me?"

"What's bothering you, Harry?"

"Evans, Lockheed and Oakley have clear beefs with Rapp, but Evans' problem is cloudy."

"Evans and Rapp are both from Baltimore on earth."

"Ya.. That tells me whatever inspired Evans goes way back. I'll see what Renie finds on her credit."

Patenaude held the side bar as we hit a rough spot in the road. But he lost his grip and slipped onto the floor. His face reddened and I tried not to laugh as he rose and held his buttocks. Still smiling, I swung my eyes to the ceiling. "I'm not laughing."

"You'd better not." I saw him grin. "Listen, my division has found no record of Evan's arrival or departure to the planet, which is odd. Only the tab at the Dillon and the rover payment. Which means she might still be in Livingston."

"I doubt it. Not if she's the killer. We need to check alternative transportation off planet. Maybe droit payments up front. Cash. Hotels in Livingston as well as transportation transactions require payment by credit since last June."

"I helped push it. It tracks people … We had a murder in the—"

"Then we have you to thank, Jahn. Perhaps, Samantha Evans was probably unaware of the change, but didn't want to miss the opportunity."

Livingston's rounded edges were tinted bronze with tiny bursts of reflected sun over the silcoplast as we passed a small crater off-road. I rubbed my mouth and moved my shoulders to "Are you going to stay the course on this one?"

With a phony grin, I raised my brows. "What I'm going to do is relax in the exercise habitat, sit in the sauna … Maybe take swim."

"And then meet the woman who you left behind ten years ago."

"Well put."

CHAPTER 7

A memo from Ariana reminded me of our dinner date. I did not plan to purchase a new succo, boots, and neckliner, but my anxiety in meeting her shook me more than I cared to admit. I rationalized my apprehension by thinking about the case. As I descended in the elevator outside the Dillon, I fought the urge to call Desmond Turcotte and officially get back aboard the investigation. My zip sounded five hundred feet above Livingston's luminescent suburban maze.

"Cobb."

"Harry, it's Jahn."

"Checking up on me, Dad?"

"I was going to do that later," he said jovially. "We have Oakley's rover. He parked it in the corner of a north end garage. Dust matches the dust on Evans' rover. And the round trip mileage is twenty-eight kilometers." Patenaude's image finally materialized over the zip window. His succo was off and his neckliner sleeves rolled up as he sat on the edge of his office desk. He had a small bandage strip on his hand and his hair was scattered.

"Cat scratch or did Gwen finally throw you out?"

Patenaude glanced at his hand. "This day has pushed me to the precipice. First, I slipped on the roverbus ride back to Livingston and bruised my back side." I tried not to make light of his troubles. "Did I hear you laugh, Harry?"

"Who me?"

"And Gwen is holding a birthday party for my granddaughter. You know how we celebrate birthdays. I forgot the cake. Then I cut my hand on the rover bubble opening. I ordered the cake she tells me she made the cake. Fortunately, it was a cheesecake base. I'll keep it at the office. Listen, I'm tired and I'm on my way home. But I want to know if you're still—"

"Investigating the murder?" I asked as the elevator reached the tree level on Avenue Seventeen. "I don't know. I keep changing my mind. Let me get through this night and I'll tell you. You're not really going to call later, are you, Jahn?"

"Nope. By the way, Mrs. Oakley, Kara Oakley, confirmed the affair with Rapp. She's a real high stepper, let me tell you. Whoa, boy … The last few months. I'll make a long story short. She used to take the weekend excursion to the Orbitus gambling halls." The elevator settled in front of Avenue Seventeen. "Rapp was a bastard. Oakley worked weekends at the plant and she was vulnerable. One side of me is glad Rapp was murdered."

"He was a bastard," I said. "Listen, I'm waiting for Renie to get back to me about Evans' credit and Max and Jody are headed to Baltimore for more background on Evans."

"I'm going to keep going after those records, too. Okay, good luck. Remember, if Ariana wasn't serious, she wouldn't have suggested the dinner."

"Agreed" I walked onto the granite sidewalk. "Good night, Jahn. Enjoy the party."

"I will. Don't stay out to late."

"Thanks, Dad."

I put away the zip and noticed I had half an hour to cross the dome by tram and meet Ariana at the Excelsior. I strolled along the sidewalk, under white street domes and spreading tree branches. Behind me, a short, stocky Asian man with slicked black hair exited through the Dillon's brass doors and appeared on the sidewalk.

Samantha Evans baffled me as I increased my pace toward the tram station. Everything Patenaude said about Evans not knowing about the new hotel and transport regulations made sense, but if she were here on Mars to murder Rapp, why would she chance leaving her name on the hotel register? What type of obsession or hatred did she harbor toward this man?

Fifty meters behind me, the heavy oriental man, whom I dubbed, Chub Chu Chub continued up the sidewalk. The glow from an approaching tram crossed over the avenue ahead. I hurried down the sidewalk and caught the escalator to my right. I tapped my fingers on the side rail and knew I would stay on the case. Once I boarded the tram, I would call Sadie. Only a few people, mostly students from the university, lingered on the platform as the sleek, white tram slowed. I placed my palm on the scanner and angled toward the open doors. I realized

Evans had used a card and not physical scans. Why not a genetic or even a palm or retinal scan?

I took a seat up front near a window screen and no longer saw Chub on the avenue sidewalk. I plugged in my zip before the tram left the station. Orbitus time was only two hours behind Livingston and Sadie turned in her office chair as she activated the office window. "Hello, Harry."

"You don't have to be working late."

"A few things I had to catch up on." She opened her green eyes wide. "Aren't we dressed to the hilt?"

"I have a dinner meeting."

"Must be quite a meeting," she said, chuckling as if she knew I was meeting Ariana, but I had only told Patenaude. "I haven't been able to locate Renie and he did say he would be … about."

"He's in the zone if his zip is off. I'll try him later."

"I was about to memo you copy of what I acquired about Samantha Evans. She was twenty-seven when she disappeared six years ago in Platinum City. October 6, 2139. No a trace of her body. Max memoed me that her brother Dan died two years ago in Baltimore."

"And don't tell me it was by pinpoint."

"No, he had a degenerative disease. Natural."

"You're sure?" I asked as the tram started.

"Yes … What is odd is the fact there was no record of disbursement of her account balances."

"Was there any reason why she would want to disappear?" I asked. "Cauldwell was a rich man and Evans was his supposedly his lover."

"Cauldwell was a rich man."

"Sadie, his life is worth looking into if we can ever pull that gutter rat, Renie, out of the zone."

Sadie winced and then shook her head. "I have talked to several establishments within the zone today and some individuals I really would not consider respectable."

The tram started above the Livingston avenues. "No, don't you call the zone, Sadie. I'll find Renie … Please go home."

"I will … when I'm done. And, Harry."

"Yes," I asked, looking out the tram.

"Enjoy your evening with Ariana."

I smiled. She waved and ended the transmission. I stared at the gray window, unplugged my zip and moved to a side seat. She was indispensable to my work and I was forever grateful she left the bureau with me when I retired. I gazed across the darkened dome. The Excelsior glowed gold within the other silhouetted buildings as the tram moved effortlessly along the smooth, white concave bed. I had a plethora of contradicting feelings, primary of which was getting involved with Ariana. Just because I happened to see her on Orbitus and was dumb enough to cross the gambling floor, didn't mean seeing her tonight or any night was a good idea.

The Excelsior's light was stronger now, enough to cast shadows in the surrounding tree parks. Like a schoolboy out on his first important date, my heart pushed against my chest and neckliner. Such predilections only lasted a few minutes, brought to a halt with the tram along the hotel's red canopy platforms. Busy busboys in green succos with narrow collars, nonexistent tails and thin lapels, loaded new arrival containments onto controller released carts with wide white wheels. The forward windows flashed the Excelsior's name, address and vacancy status, and after three short beeps, the tram operator shouted out the hotel's name.

I thought of Burroughs, a tram operator between domes, dropped by a pinpoint pulser owned by Cauldwell. The coincidences had piled up too quickly. I didn't like the fact Evans was Cauldwell's lover and then disappeared five days before his death. I moved toward the side doors and questioned whether Cauldwell really died from heart failure and I wanted to know about his credit disbursement after his death.

The doors opened quickly and I walked onto a gritty, colorful mosaic surface. I opted to parallel the mover toward the set of shiny brass doors a few dozen meters ahead. As the tram pulled from the station, I saw Chub again, this time in the third car back. I stared into his tiny dark eyes and ran along the platform. He turned as the tram moved back into the dome.

"Jahn!" I shouted into my zip, but got his memo box. "Jahn, I have a little, chubby … an Asian man trailing me."

Patenaude's voice overrode the box. "Harry."

"Jahn, I'm being trailed. You need to have somebody board the tram at Livingston."

"Are you sure?"

"Yes, damn it!"

"Short and chubby. Asian guy … I'll send somebody up to the Livingston platform from Avenue Seventeen."

"Thanks."

"Did you scan him?"

"No, I was running and tram was leaving."

"Okay … Harry: relax."

"I can't relax. Something else is going on here and I don't like it."

I shut off the zip and with clamped teeth, I backtracked along the tram platform. It was imperative I find Renie in the zone and get him back to Mars. Woman in wide green velvet dresses, bare at the shoulders, greeted me at the Excelsior's silver framed doors. I strode inside under a complex arrangement of glass crystals cascading over the upper lobby.

The walking stairs, marble with a polished ebony side rail, swept upward to the mezzanine and the Excelsior rooms. Most people gravitated to the escalator, but I needed to release my pent-up energy. The huge Roman numeral clock face, framed in gold and embedded within a venous beige facade, commenced a long, deeply resonating Westminster chime at the hour. I hope my tardiness would not weigh against me. My old supervisor in the bureau, John O'Neil, maintained people waiting always gave him the advantage.

I reached the stairway top, slightly winded. Patenaude would have pointed out my age and stamina deficiencies. I was rattled by Chub as I checked the lobby and walked along the wood paneled conference rooms toward the Excelsior's restaurant. Checking my neckliner position, I moved through the crowd and up to the front desk. The restaurant conversation mixed with a gentle piano melody. I saw a man in an apricot succo waltz his fingers across an ivory keyboard below a pearly, blue fountain.

"Sir," said a bushy haired man in a black succo.

"Harry Cobb. I have a reservation at this hour with—"

"Yes, Mr. Cobb. Miss Cervantes has arrived and has requested an alcove up front." He snapped his fingers. "Boris, please bring Mr. Cobb to Miss Cervantes' alcove."

"Thank you," I said, trying not to appear as uneasy as I felt.

Boris, his succo a velvet yellow, motioned me into the main body of the restaurant. The chandeliers in this area were dimmed and not as prodigious as the lobby fixture. He directed me to the wide, maroon carpeted stairs. I was distracted when I first saw Ariana's bare shoulders. She wore a pale blue dress, white gloves that extended to the elbows, and she had taken the time to have someone weave her dark hair, exposing her smooth white neck to a few wispy strands.

She had chosen a wide window of the Barsoom Dome, but I was not sure whether the image was direct or played back. I posted a tip in my zip with Boris's scanner. Being in a generous mood, I hit the scanner twice and he thanked me profusely. I climbed to alcove steps and had forgotten both Ariana's and the dome's natural beauty. As I gazed over the long water sheets tumbling over the rocky Gondola Falls, the sunlight danced from the window and cast a warm glow over the table linens. "She walks in beauty."

Ariana turned abruptly as if I had startled her. Her white teeth emerged under a subtle red lip shade and her dark eyes brightened. "Like the night."

I bowed graciously. "Miss Cervantes."

"Mr. Cobb," she said, gently lifting her hand upward.

I touched the fabric to my lips and sensed a slue of scents available to only those with wealth. But wealth wasn't what attracted me to her. Her beauty and charm were undeniable and irresistible assets. "You are more stunning than I remember." She smiled gradually. "And I see you have brought us via the window back to paradise."

"Paradise is closer than you think."

I walked around the table, glancing at the chateau on the cliffs and took my seat. Ariana set her elbows on the table and looked deeply into my eyes. It was enough to dazzle me and muzzle all the rehearsed lines for the evening. "Ten years …"

"It doesn't seem like ten years …"

"No, in some ways it's like I left Barsoom yesterday or last week, and conversely, ten years seems like an eternity. I was so alone."

She looked into my eyes with an unusual warmth and sincerity. "I was thirty-one years old, an aspiring socialite, occasionally dabbling in my father's company. I wanted my lifestyle and I left you alone in the dome. I'm sorry. It was my fault."

I tilted my head back and smiled. Then I held her smooth gloved hand. "That's what I always liked about you."

"What do you mean?"

"Your ability to cut to the chase I've spent the last twenty-four hours trying to unravel my feelings and you lay it on the table in ten seconds."

The waiter arrived in a white tuxedo and dark tie. He displayed the wine list on the window corner. Ariana smiled when I ordered a bottle from the Oricon Vineyard. She then excused herself and carried her matching blue purse to the restroom. I leaned back in the recliner and watched on the window as the water sheets fall into the Montero Gorge. Her perfume was still strong on the edges of my fingers.

I concentrated on her moist eyes and hair. The Rapp case, Desmond Turcotte, and potential fees or suspects were irrelevant now. A woman opened the ladies room door. In a flash I saw Ariana drop liquid from a thin tube into each eye.

Her right glove was removed. The door closed and a chill crossed my back when I thought she might use mind alternators, applied to the eyes.

The waiter placed the wine on the table as the ladies room door slid open again. I asked him to open the bottle and pour it. With an arched back and emanating elegance, Ariana moved across the main restaurant and both gloves were snugly back in place. The waiter poured the wine swiftly into the long neck glasses. I stood as she reached the stairs and checked her gait and manner. She blinked her eyes once and ascended the stairs and took my hand. I thanked the waiter and retrieved her glass.

"Thank you."

I lifted my own glass as we remained standing. Gently I clinked her glass. "To the days ahead."

"To our days."

I sipped the full-bodied Oricon and set the glass on the table. Then I seated her, but my cynicism kept me wondering about what she had dripped into her eyes. I heard the piano melody from the main room as the incandescent hebons lowered to ember tube threads and I smiled. "Remember we sang old show tunes in the chateau?"

"That was fun."

"I'm glad you decided to come to Mars, Ariana."

"Business sometimes is serendipitous."

"Have you set your business agenda?"

"Three clients here in Livingston and a half a dozen in Whittemore." I raised my brows. "Such as the responsibilities of the chairman of Amalgamated Sureties. You seemed to have moved into the role well."

"Sink or swim."

"Your father built an empire."

Her face went flat and a tiny crevice developed on her smooth brow. "My father ran this company solidly, but believe me, there were a thousand things buried when I took over. My trip here involves tying up loose ends. I don't like loose ends."

"I think that comes with change, any change. You have to be ready to look under the rug. We're all guilty of doing the same thing. I'm sure when I left the bureau the same could have been said of me."

She squeezed my hand. "You would leave your desk clean. Even the cubby-holes."

"Now what makes you say that?" I asked and finished the wine.

"Don't think father didn't look into your background after Barsoom."

"Oh, did I pass the scrutiny?"

"Of course. I didn't see the reports until after he died. You are a persistent man, Harry Cobb, but then again, I know that. And thorough. Or were, but now you are retired. So, why are you here?"

"Oh, it's a complicated case involving the Turcottes."

She closed her eyes briefly. "I know Desmond Turcotte from social gatherings in Platinum City. He really is a bore ... Did he hire you?"

The waiter climbed the mezzanine stairs. "He did, but I'm not sure what I'm going to do."

"Why would he hire you?"

"It's not important." I looked up at the waiter.

"May I show you the menu, sir?"

"Please."

The extensive listing appeared on the window. I was in the mood for real beef, but doubted whether I wanted to pay for imported cuts. "How much will a well done steak set me back?"

The waiter shined a thin red-beamed pointer at the listing, startling Ariana. "I'm sorry, Miss Cervantes. I was—"

"Quite all right."

"A steak will cost you a decidroit."

"All right."

I ordered the accompanying rice and vegetables grown fresh on Mars. Ariana wanted an organic mixture. We had just finished ordering and requested jafrin steamers when I Chub appeared near the restaurant entrance. Ariana turned. "What is it, Harry?"

"This has gone far enough." I stood quickly, threw my napkin on the table and grabbed my zip. "Excuse me, Ariana ."

Chub's face tightened and he darted toward the escalators. I scanned the front with my zip, but was sure I missed getting his image. It took me a full minute to descend the mezzanine stair and cross the restaurant. At the top of the escalator I didn't see him. "Damn.."

I played back the zip, but only saw a magnified blurred image of his dark hair and light blue succo. My first move was to request hotel security speak to me at the table and then I called Patenaude, but this time he was away from his zip, and I memoed the murky image, and reported Chub in the Excelsior. I then returned with great alacrity and apologized to Ariana for a matter of business. Her wine glass remained at the halfway level and stayed that way through our dinner conversation, which mostly centered around her.

Her many athletic talents included tennis, mountain climbing, swimming, and a intra-solar system reputation for athletic prowess. I remembered in the Barsoom Dome how she easily scaled some of the narrow mountain trails and waited for me to plod along behind. She explained about her numerous allergies. She was savvy enough to know I had watched her briefly as she applied the liquid to her eyes in the ladies room. I remained skeptical.

*   *   *   *

I chewed the last smooth beef morsel as three men in red fatigues and identity badges bounded up the mezzanine stairs. I excused myself and met them at the top. With only Chub's fuzzy picture on the zip I now gave them his physical description. The young man in charge was very cordial but I sensed he knew what I knew: Chub had long since left the hotel and disappeared within Livingston's two million residents.

I found Ariana staring into the interior of the Barsoom chateau. She looked up slowly as I returned to the table. "I want to go back to the Barsoom, Harry."

"Are you sure? I'm reticent about trying to recreate perfection."

"I've often thought of how abruptly I left that perfection. I think I was afraid."

"What were you afraid of?" I asked and leaned forward.

She raised her straight dark brows. "Commitment."

"Commitment isn't a four letter word."

"Oh, it can be if you have other unresolved things." I nodded and thought back to Chub following me on the sidewalk. My guess was he worked for Desmond and, while I didn't peg Desmond as Jason Rapp's murderer, I didn't discount his involvement, specifically with Lockheed. "I had a number of things to accomplish."

"So did I."

She smiled graciously and held my hand again. "Let's plan to go back."

I gradually exhaled. "Let me think about it."

"Afraid of commitment?"

"No, I'm afraid of ruining perfection."

Chapter 8

At two-thirty in the morning I left Ariana outside her room at the Excelsior and meandered to the external elevator. I was taken aback by her reluctance to allow me in the room. At first I thought it a feminine ploy, holding back to keep me interested or perhaps prompt me back to the Barsoom Dome. Her dark hair and eyes were vivid in my thoughts as I entered the elevator high above the darkened Livingston Dome. We had spent the last four hours on three different dance floors and our banter on and off the dance floor was exhilarating. All the old feelings were back.

I entered the elevator and turned on my zip as I started down the Excelsior's shell to the avenue. A message from Sadie and another from Patenaude, both from hours ago, flashed red on the zip. I first pushed Patenaude's message. He was seated on a sofa watching a realball game on a small window as young children ran around the room, producing a constant chatter. "Harry, I know you'll pick up this memo either early morning or maybe in tomorrow morning depending on where you end up."

"You're so smart, Jahn ..."

One of his grandkids jumped on his lap. He pointed out how a realball diamond is eleven feet longer than a major league baseball diamond on earth, but the child didn't understand. "I guess I better not tell Jenny about the fences being back fifty feet and the ball not having as much oomph ... Harry, Samantha Evans' rover produced some significant items. A tiny blue filtered eye lens and blonde hair within the t-suit."

"See, I was right."

"See, you were right" I chuckled as the elevator moved downward. "The lens contains genetic material. However, that means nothing since law does not require normal citizens, only criminals, to file genetic scans. We haven't found anything at this time, ten p.m. But the hair is not living. Either someone went in there and said she was Samantha Evans, using a facial squeeze. Appearances can be altered. Or maybe Samantha Evans needed to wear a blonde hair simulation. What we want to do is check the genetic material with any possible Evans material on file. If you're still functioning, meet me in Evans' rover garage at nine.

Oh, there's nothing I can do about your evasive, Mr. Chub, as you call him, without a clear image. But I have alerted dome security to the incident at the Excelsior. They have your zip image." He looked at his granddaughter. "And no silcoplast bats in real ball."

"Very interesting, Jahnny. I should have gone with my gut feelings." I leaned against the elevator wall and memoed him back, but asked about an Evans connection to the Turcottes or Jason Rapp.

The elevator reached ground level. I stepped onto the sidewalk and arched my back as I looked up the Excelsior's gold sheen facade. Maybe I should have pressed Ariana about staying the night. I supposed I would have time with her again in the Barsoom Dome, but a natural hesitancy loomed as I worried about her eventual return to her complicated life.

Once on the sidewalk I checked for Mr. Chub around the hotel lobby and surrounding pavilions. I pushed Sadie's memo and headed directly for the tram back to the Dillon. "Harry, I located Renie at the Lizard's Tongue in building sixty-two seventeen of the zone. He said to call anytime, but I would caution you, even though you have worked the zone, some of these people are … well you know how they are."

"I do," I said as I reached the tram escalator. Again I searched for Chub and was close to waking Desmond. Maybe an early morning call would stop his henchman from following me. I settled on sending a scathing memo informing him I did not appreciate someone following me. I stepped onto the platform and leaned against a side pole while I waited for the tram.

I entertained the theory Desmond used three people to get Rapp. Oakley and Lockheed could be pressured as employees, but the Evans connection baffled me. Evans, if she were alive, had no reason to alter her appearance, unless the reason she disappeared related to some deformity or degenerative disease. The lens was unnecessary in that scenario. Any Turcotte lackey could do that. Someone assumed and copied Evans' identity, yet no one had found a disposed facial squeeze.

When I heard the tram approach I wandered onto the smooth white platform's edge. Again, as I stared at the tram crew within the illuminated forward cabin, I thought of Burroughs, the tram operator, killed by Evans' lover's pinpoint. The doors parted and I entered an empty car. I trotted to the rear window screen, plugged in my zip and crossed the Lizard's Tongue's address into the window.

The tram pulled from the Excelsior station. I checked the charging level on my pulser and slipped it back under my succo. I didn't trust Chub or whoever hired him. Desmond was cable of doing anything to preserve Turcotte industrial presence. I set the zip scan listings for the Lizard's Tongue and made the connection. As the window gyrated with signal clutter I looked for Chub along the avenues and through the other tram cars.

On the zip window blue track lights appeared on a black ceiling and the outlines of a long bar took shape. A seedy individual with brilliant white hair smiled oddly into the scanner. His voice was modulated. "Hel-loh."

"My name is Harry Cobb, I'm trying to track down Renie Coburn."

"One droit."

"Is he there or isn't he? Why should I have to pay you any droits?"

"Droits are a magic potion. Do you wish magic, Harry Cobb, or do you wish the void?"

I reluctantly pushed an acceptance of his terms through my zip. "Now, where is he?"

"Let me locate him." The man's dark lined eyes opened wide and he smiled again. "Nice doing business with you."

I wondered if I would need to withdraw my acceptance, but figured this goof would somehow bring Renie to the window. I studied the redefined gender groups and men and woman dancing under the lights. Waitresses in electric orange short skirts crossed with trays of glowing blue glasses and mugs up to the luminescent green bar. The white haired guy returned and picked up the window scanner. The image dipped and juggled in front of me. "Oh, come on. Just pause the scanner."

I turned from the window and leaned my head on the recliner pillow. The tram continued back toward the Dillon, but even though tired, I was now charged up about the lens in the rover and the fact somebody had trailed me all evening. I only saw an area between Renie's jaw and waist at the table edge when the bar scanner was set on a table within the lounge.

His Canberra accent was heavy. "Harry?"

"Renie, I can't see you head."

"Consider yourself lucky." He reached out, his hand appearing elongated before the scanner and moved it upward. His sandy hair and bright blue eyes and the two women with magenta hair, were clear.

"Having a good time?"

"Always … I was supposed to check in with you about a murder on Mars. Guy named Rapp."

"That's right."

"I've played cards with the guy once. Five years ago at the Deco Pavilion. He was a pretty good cheater."

I leaned forward and folded my hands. "What else?"

"Liked the women. Can't fault him for that." Both ladies smiled. "I would consider him reckless."

I nodded. "Ever hear of Samantha Evans?"

"Only from Sadie. I've got calls in about her credit. I'll have something for you. She a suspect?"

"I don't know. She may have been killed," I said.

"But I have no proof of that, other than Patenaude found a lens in the rover she supposedly rented and hairs from a wig. Somebody my have been using her identity."

"Any sign of a facial alternation?"

"Nothing."

"I find it odd, mate, that the murder weapon, the pinpoint, was owned by her now deceased lover. And the other guy in the memo, Burroughs."

"Ya, that's one my reasons for my being awake," I said and crossed my legs.

"*One* of your reasons?" he asked and raised his brows up and down. "You masquerade as the nice uncle Harry. I know you. A mountain lion ready for the kill. What's your take on this, Harry, and I'll run with it."

"Two main concerns: Desmond, as in my memo, and what they're covering up over at IP-5 on Mars. I need to know what the hell it is and what Desmond is doing to cover it up. Maybe even murder. And if there is any connection between the Turcottes and Evans. Or Lockheed and Oakley."

"And Evans herself," said Renie.

"Exactly. It could take Patenaude months to get through."

"Fire me if it takes more than seventy-two hours."

I pointed at the window. "I'll hold you to it. I've got some Asian man tailing me."

"Send me an image," said Renie.

"Not available."

"Watch yourself, Harry and keep me updated."

"You watch yourself."

"The night is young, mate …"

One of the women shut off the scanner and I shook my head. The tram moved over the concave track for another ten minutes and slowed at the Dillon. I unplugged my zip and grabbed the standing rail as I gazed up at the smaller and half lit Dillon. My eyes moved across the lobby platform. The doors opened and I walked briskly outside. I touched base with hotel security about Chub and then proceeded down the escalator. I looked across the dimmed hebon lobby and was about to head to my room when my zip indicated another memo was received.

I sat on the front sofa and played back the message. Pate-naude was on an audio scan. "Harry, I assume you are preoccupied. Oakley was approached by two security men in Burlingame Park. He opened fire with his pinpoint. Both men are hurt and in field units and Oakley is missing. We have a full alert. Call me when you get this."

I raced to the window screens along the wall. While on the tram I had leaned toward Evans' complicity in Rapp's murder, but questioned the presence of Lockheed and Oakley. I attached my zip and tagged Desmond as either the formulator of the crime or an active participant. Patenaude's zip scan materialized in transit and the audio was garbled at first. The he positioned the zip.

He wore a neckliner and a red realball cap. "I didn't think I'd be hearing from you, Mr. Cobb."

"Just goes to prove you can strike out in things other than realball, Jahn. What the hell happened with Oakley?"

"I don't know why he was in the park, but the son of a bitch opened fire on two of our men. I think they're going to make it, but I'm not sure. Hardly the actions of an innocent man."

"Maybe a cornered man," I said, wishing I had his jafrin cup in my own hand. "Where is he now? He must be here in the dome somewhere."

"Who knows? I'm on my way back from the field unit. My question revolves around his presence here at all. Why would he hang around Livingston?"

"That's a good point. I think he was scared, Jahn. He must know the scuttlebutt around the dome."

Patenaude picked up the huge red and blue mug, and sipped the jafrin. He smacked his lips. "I have to go with facts. I can't be going off on wild theories. And the damned fact is Oakley stalked Rapp with a pinpoint and traveled down the connector road to IP-7. He had the motive. Rapp had the affair with his wife."

"I agree," I said and yawned. "I need a cup of that brew. Listen, he probably wanted to kill Rapp and I can't say I blame him, but that doesn't mean he *did* kill Rapp. With the storm."

"He had a pinpoint."

"Was it Cauldwell's pinpoint?" I asked loud enough for the desk clerk to turn. "Well?"

"We don't know where he got the pinpoint. So, you can't say categorically, Harry, he didn't kill Rapp."

I sat back in the recliner and folded my arms. Then I unbuttoned my succo and pointed at Patenaude. "Jahn, we don't know he didn't do it either. Evans and Lockheed—"

"I have to present the facts."

"He acted guilty firing at your guys. Where the hell is Lockheed?"

Patenaude held the jafrin mug, but didn't drink. "You know you're a pain in the ass, Harry?"

"I know that."

"I will lock up Oakley if I find him and I will charge him."

"You do what you have to do. I'm pursuing the Evans angle with my people."

He set the cup in the side holder when his zip sounded.

"I'm going to get some sleep."

"I'll second that." I watched as Patenaude's face tightened, but I couldn't understand the audio. "Okay, Jahn, nighty night."

"Wait … Harry, wait. "He nodded and shut off the memo. "You sleep on this little tidbit. The Evans t-suit. Ripped at the forearm. That's how I hurt my hand on the jagged piece of metal on that rover."

I had stood up but sat back down. "You rip a t-suit in those temperatures and you'll have cold burn to write home about."

"Where's Evans and what does she have to do with this?"

I rubbed my eyes. "At this point, Jahn. I don't care. Let her flee the planet, the solar system. I don't care. Let Oakley take over the dome. I'm going to sleep."

"No mind."

"Funny man. Good night." I tore the zip from the window and marched across the lobby. The elevator was at lobby level. Longing for sleep, I stepped inside and started up along the building in the darkness.

CHAPTER 9

I fell face down on the bed and didn't bother to change into a night suit. The blood rushed to my head and I felt as if I were sinking into the bed's air cushion. I verbally commanded the hebons to dim slowly. Darkness surrounded me and I reminded myself I had tripled the security checks on the room. Chub's sneaky countenance infiltrated my drifting thoughts and nebulous color blasts swarmed inside my eyes. A zip memo sounded as I went out.

"Hebons on," I said without thinking. The ensuing brightness and my aching eyes caused me to second guess the impulsive decision. "Hebons off."

I pushed the flashing red bulb and the audio crackled. Renie's Australian accent penetrated the darkness. "Harry, old buddy. I can tell you the reports about Cauldwell's pulser are verified. Cauldwell was a successful investment creditier and a confirmed bachelor in Platinum City for thirty-five years. Record from a field unit in the Carnes section of Platinum City stated he died of a heart attack, but I did find an addendum, originally deleted from the official record. A dissenting doctor wanted to look into a possibility of a high frequency disruption because of minute tissue variations. Somebody squelched it. Good luck in finding those reports, mate."

"Then he was murdered. And Evans was gone."

"I will, however, give it a shot. Gem number two: And your not going to like this one." The memo paused.

"I just want to go to sleep," I said into the darkness.

"Your friend Ariana." I opened my eyes, but didn't order the hebons on. "She and Cauldwell. They were close … They physically close, Harry."

"Come on." Sweat collected on my forehead and I manually turned on the hebons. "No …"

"I'm headed to Platinum City right now to snoop. Give me a memo if you're off the case or don't want me to go any further."

I didn't know if the tears in my eyes were from jealousy or because Ariana had just catapulted into my suspect grouping. Perhaps, it was the hour and my state of exhaustion. I tried to convince myself Renie's memo was different from what I just heard. I played it back one time while I was in bed and another time when I went to the liquor cabinet and poured myself a respectable glass of Scotch.

"She was once his lover and so was Evans. Evans disappeared and Cauldwell died." I lifted the Scotch to my tongue and set the glass on the table. Maybe I was reading too much into this. My gut feeling, always the best barometer, told me Evans was dead and Ariana snatched her credit. "No. She's independently wealthy. She just wouldn't need Evans' credit."

I knew where this was leading as I plugged my zip into the hotel room window and requested a bureau background check on Ariana. Whether I denied it or not, my next step would be a check of Orbitus records for either Ariana or Evans' shuttle payments. To kill Rapp, Ariana would need to have arrived on Mars a day earlier than she had claimed. My attention was drawn to an early picture of Ariana taken in 2120. At nineteen, her face was thin and her dark hair straighter, but her eyes still possessed an immeasurable beauty I found difficult to resist.

Her resume was perfect; an outstanding grade performance supplementing her remarkable social standing in earth boarding schools and Aaronson College in Enfield, Massachusetts. Before assuming the position of controlling officer of Amalgamated Sureties, her activities were mostly social and charitable. Her father died from heart failure and I immediately linked his death to Cauldwell, but I smiled for thinking such things. I wondered, as I stared at dozens of social posted photographs, how I could think she was masquerading as Evans and capable of murder. She was shorter, but could have used a disguise.

"But why would she kill Rapp? That is the more relevant question."

I brought the Orbitus records onto my window. She left the hotel yesterday via a midday shuttle and arrived at the Excelsior around five. Unless she bolted from the murder scene back to Orbitus, my theory was meaningless. I scanned every shuttle departure and arrival on Orbitus and saw neither Ariana's nor Evans' name. Then I buried my head on my crossed forearms next to the Scotch glass and descended into sleep.

*   *   *   *

A whooshing sound awakened me within the building silcoplast span's gray light. For a short time I didn't know where I was nor why the noise increased in intensity. Before I oriented myself, I was cognizant an inverted pulser was somewhere inside the room. I tripped over the recliner and scrambled to my feet as I ordered on the hebons. The lights blazed as I scanned, but an inverted pulser diverts every other sound and I quickly realized, as I covered my ears from the howling barrage, I was not going to find this pulser.

I grabbed my zip and raced toward the door. Using the master code, I destabilized all three locks, but the door did not slide open. The noise battered my eardrums as I clawed at the door edges and prayed I could open the door before the inversion. Someone had added more codes. I removed my own pulser and fired a steady red beam at the door, not even denting the surface as the pain tightened in my ears. "Damn you!"

I scrambled across the room, and fell a number of times during the increasing crescendo. I held my ears as I approached the panel covering the clear silcoplast. The panel moved effortlessly across the track, revealing a smattering of dome lights far below. I fired the beam in a circle and then kicked the transparency away. The cooler night air pushed into the room and I crawled onto a protruding support beam sixty floors above Avenue Seventeen.

I slowly turned to gain the most minimal grip, waiting for the pulser to invert. Air currents moved quickly at this height and my stomach was overcome with an anxious feeling reserved for such life and death situations. The gushing pulser waves pushed through the silcoplast hole as I precariously shuffled down the ledge. Several times, I fought to keep my balance on the thin silcoplast protrusion.

I was less than ten meters down the berm when the sound ceased. That meant five seconds to the inversion. I counted down the seconds and clawed my fingers around the building joints as I scurried away. I braced for massive explosion.

An instant burst of orange, heat filled smoke pushed out the room silcoplast like the tail of a twentieth century rocket nozzle. I held on with my fingers and my foot swung into the air. I quickly repositioned myself on the solid beam. The explosion was over as quickly as it had burst into the night. I instantly surmised I was saved only by the rigid room construction, designed mostly against a spreading fire, which produced a safe room shell around a vulnerable silcoplast span.

Alarms sounded inside the hotel. I closed my eyes, knowing I was not out of danger until I actually got back inside the Dillon. The upper intense hebons popped on. I closed my eyes when I saw the building facade down to the avenue. I slowly dragged my foot back and kicked the next room's silcoplast, but the resulting thud was not loud enough to draw attention. With my left hand, I looped my arm down and rapped on the surface. Bright light appeared on rooms beyond my own destroyed room. I placed my left hand back on the upper frame and felt my raised zip board until I found the lower security frequency. I pushed the button, fully aware of the deadly drop behind me.

CHAPTER 10

A hovering tracer nudged to my position on the Dillon's sixtieth floor. Two security men yanked me away from the ridge and into the warmer and brighter tracer. They moved me to a side transport bed and the tracer sped, against my wishes, to a field unit. Fatigue and anxiety forced me into a light sleep on the way. When I opened my eyes, I was connected to life scanners and nutrient pushers in my arm. Because I had come so close to dying, I reluctantly put up with their procedures.

I heard Patenaude's voice in the hall and he quickly roun-ded the corner. "You'll go to any length for attention, Harry."

"What time is it?" I asked in a groggy voice and then rubbed my itchy eyes.

"One-thirty."

"Great … I hate heights, Jahn."

"I know."

"Who tried to kill me?" I asked and stared at the perforated white ceiling tiles.

"Someone who does not want you to dig into Rapp's murder."

"Thanks, I was able to deduce that." I pinched the top of my nose. "Ever been trapped sixty floors up against the outside wall of a building?"

"Can't say that I have … What are you complaining about, you finally got some sleep."

I grinned, but kept my eyes closed. "My zip is in the drawer. There's a memo from Renie."

Patenaude waddled to the center cabinet. "By the way, I called Sadie. She says she's glad you survived, but she was afraid she wasn't going to be droit credited this week."

I smiled again. "I'm glad to hear my threatened demise has such dire consequences."

Patenaude slid open the drawer and removed the zip. He sat in the side recliner and listened with me to Renie's accented voice bring Ariana into the investigation. When the transmission ended, he was silent for a few moments. "Don't draw any erroneous conclusions."

I finally propped myself up on the pillows. "I don't like coincidences. Coincidences tap into my cynical nature."

"So, she was Cauldwell's lover."

"I'm connecting the dots with Burroughs's death and the pinpoints tied to Cauldwell and his other lover, Samantha Evans, who supposedly rented that rover. I've checked the shuttle flights between Orbitus and Mars. Unless she had a private craft and rented the rover with a disguise—"

"The woman on the rental playback is five foot seven. Ariana is five foot two," said Patenaude. "The face would have to be altered."

"And that woman has blonde hair! What about the lens? We'll do a genetic scan."

"No you won't because the lens is missing."

"What? Come on.... I'm telling you the guy that was following me last night is responsible for the pulser inversion and he probably grabbed the lens."

"You're upset, Harry."

"You're damned right I'm upset! I know when somebody is tracking me down. You have to find this guy. I can't believe Ariana is involved in this at all."

"Wait, there is one way to test your theory. Ariana's arm would be severely injured. Remember the tear in the t-suit?"

I shook my head. "Not if the tear occurred back in the garage, Jahn. You're assuming it happened out in the desert." I thought back to last night and how she had removed her right glove in the ladies room. "She wore *gloves* last night at dinner, Jahn."

"Then we're going to simply have to question her and check all private flights to the planet ... Is she capable of such daring and timing? To track down Rapp like that and then return to Orbitus?"

"Hell, I don't know. She had an opportunity to kill Rapp when they were both on Orbitus the night before."

"Orbitus is a crowded place," said Patenaude. He set my zip back in the drawer. Then he looked over his shoulder. "Where is she now?"

I pushed my lips together. "Let me handle this."

"That would not be in the regs."

"Who the hell cares about regs?" I closed my eyes for a second. "She's on a business trip to Whittemore. I'll take the tram over there and talk to her. But I have to ask *the* pertinent question: Why would she kill Rapp?"

Patenaude stroked his chin and shook his head. "I need some jafrin."

I slid my feet over the bed and stood. I pulled back the connecting green fabric on the field unit treatment suit. "I'm getting the hell out of here and over to Whittemore."

"There are monitor lines attached to that suit."

"Good. Maybe they'll think I'm dead."

Patenaude moved closer. "Harry, don't forget our friend Mr. Oakley and the shoot-out last night. And Lockheed is missing. You have a vested interest here. You know what happens to judgment in cases like this."

I stared into his blue eyes. "I appreciate your concern, Jahn. But I have to find the truth, no matter where it leads."

Chapter 11

I slept most of the six hours to the Whittemore Dome, located on the edge of a shadowed crater in western Elysium Planitia. I constantly checked for Chub as I left the tram. He must have planted the pulser and probably had left the planet by now. I stared through the silcoplast, as did rafts of tourists at the overlook, into the crater's shadowed rim. Theories about the Rapp murder bobbed within my head, producing a general agitation and uneasiness I didn't like.

Along the ramp the sunlight dabbed the rusty crater rocks. I was no closer to absolving Ariana of complicity in Rapp's murder than when I left Livingston. Nor could I discount Desmond Oakley sharing the cover up. My zip beeped and the window indicated Max had memoed from earth. I picked up my containment and walked over to the windows lining the retaining wall. In the afternoon sunshine, I connected to the earth frequency. Max and Jody were in a hotel room overlooking Baltimore's skyline.

"Max."

"I just got the word from Sadie, Harry. Are you all right?"

"Unscathed."

"You do not appear damaged," said Jody.

"Ever the tactful one," said Max, rolling his eyes.

"I do not possess your ability to confabulate," she said.

"Try it sometime, you'll like it."

I moved my hands. "Whoa. Whoa. Hold it … What is your status?"

Max stepped in front of Jody. "Samantha Evans' brother reported her missing when she failed to return from a trip to Platinum City and the Vegas Colony.

The story about blood on the sidewalk was bogus. That was six years ago, October. Brother is dead."

"October the sixth," said Jody.

Max's mouth twisted. "Right."

"Evans was just missing and never turned up?"

"She never turned up … My plan, Harry, is to do some background work on Rapp and Evans here in Baltimore. I also have more detailed requests in on Ariana."

"I'm not sure that's a good idea."

"Harry, we need to know if she had a reason to kill Rapp."

"And I would suggest a link between Rapp and Evans," said Jody.

"We don't know that," said Max. "It's possible only because they're both from Baltimore."

"I'm heading to a little hotel here called the Dunstable. I plan to confront Ariana."

"Be careful," said Max. "What about Renie?"

"He's looking into the credit thing, why Evans' credit exists, yet she hasn't been seen in six years."

"There's a link," said Max.

"Find it."

I cut the zip and pulled it from the window. The Whittemore Dome reflected the reduced Martian sun. I chose to walk the full kilometer to the dome. While I was dozing on the tram, I had wondered about Ariana and the torn t-suit. I could not remove images of her white gloves from my mind, nor could I forget the incriminating peak at her bare arm through the open door. A cold burn arm would nail her for the murder of Jason Rapp.

* * * *

A short conversation with Patenaude reminded me Lockheed, who stuffed his t-suit into an IP-7 eliminator after following Rapp into the desert, had not yet surfaced. I could explain his ditching the suit, and strongly felt Desmond had granted him shelter somewhere within the Turcotte properties. I ambled from the tram platform above a compact arboretum on the outskirts of the dome. I had mixed feelings about Oakley. His shooting of the security men seemed more than an act of fear, but I didn't know his personality well enough. So, I left myself a memo to follow up.

The buildings and sprawl were more apparent behind the arboretum trees. Whittemore was overbuilt and I preferred the well-planned land preservation at Livingston. I knew I risked nixing the rekindled relationship with Ariana if I asked her directly about Samantha Evans. After scanning hotel records on my zip and I found Ariana had booked a conference patio the Pelican Resort. An hour later, I located her with three clients at the top of a long, musty wooden staircase. The patio was nestled within an array of green hebons and tropical plants from earth. She was dressed casually in khaki slacks, a blue jersey, unbuttoned at the top and brown hiking boots. The resort maps showed some hiking trails, but I figured her attire was purely ornamental.

My heart pounded quicker than during my harrowing experience on the ledge. As I finally skirted the round glass table, I watched her animated dialogue with two women and a man. She first saw me out of the corner of her eye and initially appeared shocked, but recovered instantly with a huge smile. "Harry, my God."

"I'm sorry to disturb you, Ariana."

She stood and approached me quickly. I was surprised when she thrust her arm around me. "Everyone. This is my good friend, Harry Cobb."

I gazed at her arm, but didn't see any scratches or abrasions.

"I do apologize."

"No need to. Please join us."

"Oh, no. I don't want to disturb a business meeting. I merely wanted to let you know I'm over here."

She maintained a wide smile, but I sensed it was a cover. Both her first reaction to my presence and her patronizing attitude concerned me. I sensed a confrontation when she asked her guests indulgence and steered me across the fieldstone. "I must say I am just slightly surprised to see you here."

"Why is that?" I asked, noting her annoyance with me.

"I thought we agreed to meet on my return."

"You don't want to se me?" I asked.

Her voice was now tight and tense. "You didn't answer my question: Why are you here?"

"Do you know Samantha Evans?"

The question hit her like an opening artillery barrage of an important battle. Her brow creased. "Samantha was a tramp. She moved in on my relationship with Henry Cauldwell. She lost. I won."

"I see."

"Why the hell would you show up here and ask me that?"

I didn't know how far I could push the questioning. "I'm investigating the death of a man named Jason Rapp." I waited for a reaction, but she looked confused. "He was murdered with Cauldwell's pinpoint pulser."

"I never heard of Jason Rapp. In fact, I'm taken aback, Harry. You wine and dine me and try and get something going again ... Just for the sake of your damned investigation?"

"That is not true."

"Appearances would indicate that. Why don't you head back to Livingston and leave me alone?"

Again, I scrutinized the skin on her right arm. Maybe the t-suit ripped after she left the desert or when she entered the rover. Perhaps, she wasn't involved in the Rapp murder at all and I had just jeopardized my chances with her. I didn't apologize as she faced the table. My intuition told me she was still a suspect. "What do you know about Cauldwell's pinpoint pulser?"

She stopped, but didn't turn for a few seconds, and then marched rapidly toward me. "You're a son of a bitch."

"Maybe I am."

"You are! I figured you more than a low life gumshoe. I don't carry a pulser and if I did it wouldn't be Henry Cauldwell's pulser because Henry Cauldwell is dead, but you probably already know that. And as far as self-defense—I have a spray block. You want to see it?"

"No."

"Good-bye, Harry. Enjoy the rest of your life!"

She stomped back to the table. No one said anything nor flinched as she sat. A few seconds later, the older man to her left leaned forward. "Does this mean we shouldn't change our policies?"

"We'll talk business later," she said, looking over her shoulder at me.

Her dark eyes touched me for a moment before I pivoted toward the escalator, but her defensive posture unnerved me. I descended the escalator and questioned why she had so easily volunteered information about Cauldwell. I had seen criminals ratchet up interrogations when they were aware I already possessed facts. Salesmen used that tactic to overcome objections to products. I gazed over my shoulder toward the patio garden. She had not only had admitted to knowing Evans, but even claimed she somehow beat her in some odd lover's competition.

I walked off the escalator quickly, entered an alcove with several windows, and plugged in my zip, but tightened my face when I looked upstairs. I was mysteriously in love with Ariana and had just circuitously accused her of murdering Jason Rapp and she knew it.

Inside the window, Patenaude appeared at a restaurant with Gwen amidst tables of patrons and darting waiters. "I apologize."

"I'm used to it, Harry, after twenty-five years," said Gwen, her white hair styled perfectly.

"You're looking good tonight, Gwenny."

"For the price I paid for that hair set, she should look nice," said Patenaude with a smile.

"Stop it, you," said Gwen.

"What's up, Harry?"

I swallowed and tried to gather my thoughts. The image of Ariana in the Excelsior restroom stuck like an advertisement banner in my head. "I just confronted Ariana about the Rapp murder."

"What did she say?"

"She admitted up front to knowing Evans and being Cauldwell's lover; well not in so many words."

Patenaude nodded and leaned toward the window. "I can't get Samantha Evans' credit records without a court order."

"I have Renie using his sources … I'm a little sick of the Turcottes behavior in this. I should say Desmond."

"I know. I'm scheduled to meet with him in the morning. I want to know what went on in IP-5."

I pounded the table. "You're damned right. At the minimum! He's hiding Lockheed, I'd bet my life on it. As far as Oakley goes, he needs to answer questions because he was aware enough of the IP-5 foul-ups and concerned enough to tell his wife."

Patenaude pointed his finger and squinted. "I think Oakley wanted Rapp dead because of the affair with his wife. Oakley is a hard working, emotional guy with a temper."

Ariana and her clients moved down the escalator. "What makes you think he didn't kill Rapp?"

I talked to Patenaude, but stared at the escalator. "The pulser. How would he get Cauldwell's pulser?"

Ariana gabbed and looked relaxed. I faced Patenaude. "I want you to check shuttle records around the time Burroughs was killed."

"I did. Nothing on Evans and, I'm sorry, nothing on Ariana."

"I'd like to talk to that Desmond myself. Just because the Turcottes own half the planet, transport lines and solar system investment …"

"That's a mouthful," said Patenaude as the waitress brought him a mammoth piece of strawberry glazed cheesecake.

"What I said or the cheesecake?"

"Both. I'm calling the bureau if Desmond doesn't start talking."

"I have to call Max," I said as Ariana moved less than ten meters away through the lobby, but didn't see me tucked in the alcove. "I want to know more about Amalgamated Sureties. Who works for her? What things have they invested in …"

"How about a connection to IP-5?" asked Patenaude and then he pushed a smooth piece of cheesecake into his mouth.

"Good point. Desmond and Ariana know each other socially."

"I check on my end, too."

"I'll let you two enjoy the rest of your meal."

"Take care, Harry," said Gwen.

"And stay away from any inverted pulsers."

"Oh, I just love walking along a one meter ledge sixty stories up. Keeps me on my toes. Good night."

I leaned out of the alcove. Ariana and her people entered the central elevator and the doors closed. My gut told me to tail her, but my heart told me to leave her alone. I memoed Sadie with a general update and request for information about Amalgamated Sureties. For a few seconds I weighed my options and decided to stay at Whittemore.

* * * *

Working on a tip from the hotel desk clerk, I located Ariana three hours later. She sat at a booth window inside a dimly lit bar a few blocks from the hotel. Amplifiers were illegal when used without a court permit. I risked prosecution when I activated the little disk in my ear. A man named Miller was spewing out figures like a ship's ion trail. I, at first thought he was an accountant, but soon surmised a closer relationship with Ariana. She chatted with him in a lower voice as if she had known him awhile. I noted nothing of significance and backed away from her world of figures, investment and policy numbers.

Less than ten minutes later, she pranced down the avenue away from her hotel. I followed at a discrete distance and wondered why she quickly ascended the tram steps. I hid behind shrubs until she reached the top platform and then I hopped onto the opposite escalator. She paced quickly at the Livingston tram connection. I immediately memoed the front desk to ship my containment back to the Dillon and I secured a Livingston ticket on my credit scan.

The Livingston tram hummed to the platform ten minutes later. I opted to enter through the rear section, eight cars behind Ariana. When I settled into my recliner, I plugged my zip into the window and called the field unit between the Dillon and the Excelsior. The tram smoothly exited the platform and crossed the darkened dome. Within ten minutes, we had left the dome and traversed the shadowed, rock covered plain.

I checked with the field unit playback storage and used a considerable amount of charm to cajole the personnel. They scanned for anyone who had come to the unit within the past forty-eight hours for treatment of a cold burn, but no one was recently treated a cold burn. I leaned back in the recliner, shut off the overhead hebon and shook my head. I still suspected Ariana, but had to prove whether she left Orbitus or was on the colony when Rapp was killed. I needed to track her exact movements, but I also wanted checks from Patenaude on the private flights to and from Orbitus.

I scanned listings for other field units inside Livingston and from the middle of the darkened desert placed a call to a little facility on Livingston's fringe. A late shift attendant informed me that a blonde haired woman came in two nights ago for a cold burn injury. "What color eyes?" I asked, thinking of the lens found in the rover.

"I don't know, but I do know she was burned near the wrist and received a beveled surgery graft, only visible with magnifiers.

"Name of patient."

"Says here, Wanda Mullen … paid in droits."

"Was a genetic sample taken?"

"No, sir."

"Damn." I stroked my bristly chin.

I would gain nothing unless I actually walked up eight cars and placed a magnifier over Ariana's wrist. Going to a remote facility, under an assumed name, and paying with droits was clever and perfect way to alleviate the unanticipated wrist injury. A court edict could order a magnifier scan, but I also knew Patenaude would have little chance of obtaining the edict quickly.

I memoed Sadie after I did a negative preliminary check on the name Wanda Mullen. Although I believed the name usage purely spontaneous, I wanted Max and Renie to use their sources. I slouched in the tram recliner's fallow light and constructed a scenario in my head that allowed Ariana to kill Rapp. I assumed she had left Orbitus on a private flight, and I attributed the rented rover, to a miscalculation. She erroneously thought trams were available to chase Rapp into the desert and she believed she could anonymously rent a rover, using droits. Nor could she anticipate the cold burn. Somehow, she returned inconspicuously to Orbitus and resumed her normal business activities. In a court of law, I would need witnesses to corroborate her day on Orbitus. But getting her to court required evidence and suspicion of wrongdoing. All I had right now was speculation.

* * * *

At three in the morning, I was awakened by the deceleration beeps and I immediately sprang from my recliner. I stumbled down the aisle and held the side rail outside down the tram steps. Interrogating Ariana was the only way to find the truth. I left the tram, crossed the empty platform and glanced at the half lit Livingston buildings, but my main concern was Ariana's pending departure from the tram. I slipped behind one of the white support poles and rubbed my lips against my beard stubble as I waited for the passengers to disembark.

After a few minutes it was readily apparent she was still on the tram. I bounded back up the stairs into last car and slid past an old man sleeping down back. A young woman glanced at me as I passed. The next car was empty, but through the side silcoplast, I saw Ariana enter the enclosed port elevator. She was safely inside and rising above the platform before I could leave the car. Was she heading to the port? With the meeting in Whittemore, it was possible her business was complete. To leave in the middle of the night after a confrontation with me was unusual. I thought about calling Patenaude or perhaps even trailing her, but Patenaude could do little without evidence. If she was hiding something, I was helpless to find it.

CHAPTER 12

I walked briskly into security station fifteen at four p.m., after sleeping long enough for my overnight containment to arrive from Whittemore. Patenaude told me Oakley was arrested by Kranz and his zealous troopers inside a small hotel at the southern dome only minutes after my arrival at the Livingston platform. Some question remained as to whether Kranz had roughed him up on the way to the detention rooms. Oakley had specifically requested a Turcotte lawyer, which I found interesting, and refused all cooperation with Patenaude's investigation. I memoed Sadie about the Oakley arrest and popped into Patenaude's office.

Patenaude sat on the edge of his desk and gripped his jafrin mug. "Desmond has personally dispatched one of Alton Bardsley's people to handle Oakley's case."

"Then there's more to this than Oakley firing at those two security people. There has to be ..."

"One would think so, but we might not be seeing this level of activity if Rapp hadn't been killed on Turcotte property."

"Jahn, I still say they can hide Lockheed and there's nothing we can do about it."

Patenaude rounded the desk to his beeping desk window.

"Here's that information on Ariana."

"And there's where the trouble lies. I'd stake my life she walked into that field unit and paid in droits for the cold burn."

"What the hell do you want me to do? Arrest her and scan the arm?"

"Ya." I smiled and so did he. "What have you got?"

"Okay, Ariana traveled under her own name to Orbitus this morning and she wasted no time in boarding a ship to Platinum City."

"Sure, she's going home."

Patenaude looked at the window one more time and again sat on the edge of his desk. "Look, Harry. Don't think I'm discounting what you've told me about Ariana. I find the damned Evans thing bizarre." He counted on his thumb and fingers. "Number one: Evans disappearing completely is convenient to somebody. Number Two: Ariana shared Evans' lover, Cauldwell, the owner of the pinpoint that killed Rapp and Burroughs. That stirs the pot further. I've had the zip scan for common things between Rapp and Burroughs, but I have come up with absolutely nothing."

"I understand that, Jahn."

"And the Evans credit request is stalled in the courts because of overlapping jurisdiction."

"Renie will break through that."

"Renie has served time in various detention confines on three occasions," said Patenaude, crossing his arms.

"That's why he works for me. I tell him what I want and he gets it."

"Careful you don't get yourself into trouble. "His zip sounded. "Yes, what is it?"

"Inspector, Mrs. Oakley has arrived in the detention confine."

"Thank you." He shut off the memo and faced me. "You want to talk to her?"

"Sure, I want to talk to her and I want to talk to Desmond directly at the Turcotte Dome."

"Yes, I understand that. We'll see what he makes of our request. Come on, let's go. Get ready for this one."

* * * *

Mrs. Oakley had short dark hair and a tall, lean frame, accentuating her tight blue body suit. Her bedroom eyes sent out signals of availability and I understood how she could easily reel in a cad like Rapp, especially inside an Orbitus gambling room, hours away from her husband on the planet. She looked me over. Patenaude seemed taken aback when she took his hand and her low voice only added to her persona. "Inspector, I'm afraid I started all this."

Patenaude pulled back his hand and glanced down the hall.

"Mrs. Oakley—"

"Kara."

"Kara." He turned. "Do you have a lawyer or are you getting a lawyer?"

"Jim's getting a Turcotte lawyer," she said, checking me out.

"What I'm saying, you may want legal counsel before I start asking you questions."

Her eyelids dipped as she spoke slowly and rather seductively. "I am perfectly capable of speaking for myself." She ran her fingers along Patenaude's shirt cuff.

"No doubt, you are. Why don't you tell me about Jason Rapp."

I noted she did not seem affected by her husband's arrest.

"Jason was a unique individual. He gave me nights of … *pleasure*."

"Then you did have an affair with him."

"Oh, yes, yes. Affair is a minimal description of what he could do."

"That's nice," said Patenaude. "Then your official statement is you had an affair with Jason Rapp."

"Officially, yes."

I stepped forward and tried not to follow the body suit curves. "Mrs. Oakley, what did you tell Jason Rapp about problems in Turcotte plant number five?"

She furrowed her smooth brow and Patenaude pointed at me. "This is Harry Cobb, a private investigator. He's with me."

"What aspect of me would you like to investigate, Mr. Cobb?" she asked and pushed her fingers up through her hair, tightening the body suit fabric around her chest. I had dealt with too many coy little flirts in my career. "Well?"

"Why don't you start by answering my damned question," I said loudly.

Her eyes widened and her voice was reduced to a more civil tone. "Jim told me night after night they were in big trouble."

"How so?"

"IP-5 refines ore for shipment around the solar system," she said.

"We're well aware of the plants functions," I replied.

"What happened that Jason Rapp was able to blackmail your husband? He did blackmail your husband, didn't he, Mrs. Oakley?"

"Yes, he did."

I nodded and moved closer to the long body suit. "Just what the hell was happening in that plant?"

"You don't have to answer that," said Kranz, sticking his oversized head around the corner and burst inside. He was followed by a more formal man with silky gray hair and clad in a green succo with yellow trim and buttons. "I have a Turcotte lawyer here with me, Kara. You say nothing."

"Why don't you let her decide that," I said as my fist clamped.

"May I go?" she asked.

"I have no further questions," said Patenaude.

She pressed her thin lips as left the room as if she were walking down the stage of a beauty pageant. The woman was trouble and I was glad she was gone.

Kranz seemed more sure of himself. Maybe it was the presence of the lawyer. His eyes twinkled when he spoke. "I will defer all inquiries to counsel Emmons."

"Any alleged Turcotte business dealings are to be handled in a purely legalistic forum," said Emmons.

"Spoken like a true lawyer. Did you ever think what happened at IP-5 might have some bearing on this murder investigation?" I asked.

"I have no comment at this time," said Emmons.

I thought him aloof, sarcastic, but competent. "Do you work directly for Alton Bardsley?"

"I am part of the Bardsley team, yes."

I nodded at Patenaude. "I see. I want to speak with Oakley."

"That's a good idea," said Patenaude.

"I'm afraid Mr. Oakley will have nothing to say to you," said Emmons

I now moved directly up to Emmons and peered into his hazel, blood-shot eyes. "You're part of the Turcotte team. Has Mr. Oakley requested your representation?"

"Mr. Oakley is a Turcotte employee, sir."

"So what?"

"Are you an official here? Because if you are not, I would advise that you not harass my client."

Patenaude left the room and chatted on his zip as he paced in the outer office. My frustration with Desmond and his legal drones mounted. "You tell Desmond I want to see him."

Emmons squinted. "I suggest you handle any communications with Mr. Turcotte."

"You've got a damned answer for everything, do you?"

Patenaude appeared in the doorway. "Mr. Emmons only represents Turcotte business interests via Mr. Bardsley. I would advise him to respond to Mr. Cobb's questions in a more ethical and forthright manner."

"I will officially protest this in any court proceeding."

"We'll worry about court proceedings when they occur," said Patenaude.

Emmons' face flattened, but his eyes darted between Pate-naude and me. He picked up his containment case and exited the room, followed by Kranz. Patenaude motioned with his head and we veered into the side corridor.

"Jahn, I'm heading over to the Turcotte Dome when we're done here. I'm sick of this nonsense."

"I don't blame you, Harry."

We entered a small elevator, cleared security and traveled down three floors to the narrow detention corridor. Rows of white lattice bars covered the individual detention cells. The sandy haired Oakley sat in the corner cell. He was a rangy man, clad now in a yellow detention suit and dark boots. His chiseled face had age lines around an angled nose.

"Scanners on," said Patenaude and red lights glowed on the cell window scanner frames. "Mr. Oakley. I have Harry Cobb here. He's working with me on the Rapp murder. You have the right to counsel and the right against self-incrimination."

"Mr. Emmons said he would represent my interests, but I didn't officially hire him," said Oakley in a clear voice. A strict pronunciation of his R's indicated he either was born on Mars or had worked here a long time. He gazed at the overhead scanner. "What do you want to know, Mr. Cobb?"

I held the lattice. "Did you kill Rapp?"

"No, but I wanted to …"

"You were out there, you fled and you shot two Livingston security men. The evidence is overwhelming."

Oakley's Adam's apple moved up and down as he swallowed and approached the lattice. "The man was involved with my wife. I caught my wife talking to him on her zip. I monitor all her zip communications."

"I'm not surprised,." I said.

"Rapp's plan was to meet with Lockheed and then rendezvous with Kara at Livingston. I knew when he was landing on the Orbitus shuttle. I followed him into the desert. Right to IP-5 where I work. A bad storm was brewing. He spoke with Joe and then left on the IP-7 connector. And, Ya, I followed them out there."

"Them?" asked Patenaude.

"Joe left right after Rapp … into the dust storm."

I crossed my arms. "Then where the hell is Lockheed? Did he kill Rapp?"

"Desmond must have him tucked away somewhere so he doesn't have to answer any of the IP-5 questions."

"You think he killed Rapp? Rapp was blackmailing him because of your wife told him something was wrong in IP-5. I'm convinced Rapp's knowledge of the problem was minimal, but his ability to con people was unmatched."

"You're right, Mr. Cobb, Kara only knew we were having problems out there and Joe was in the middle of it."

I glanced at Patenaude. He cleared his throat and faced Oakley. "Tell us about those problems."

"That, gentlemen, I cannot do. Mr. Emmons has requested I not address those issues."

"Oh, come on," I said and threw up my hands as I turned away from the lattice. "Damn it, Oakley, we're trying to find out why Rapp was murdered, although at this point I see no reason to continue on this case."

"Desmond hired you according to Emmons."

I turned but didn't walk back. "That's about ready to come to it's appropriate end."

Oakley now gripped the lattice near Patenaude. "Mr. Cobb, I wanted to kill him and if the storm hadn't been so bad, I probably would have killed him, but I didn't!"

Now I approached him. "Then why did you shoot the security men?"

"They went after me on orders from Kranz. I had no choice and I'm not stupid. I heard what happened to Rapp. My plan was to leave the planet."

"My advice," I said as I exhaled. "My advice is to get yourself a private lawyer. You have everything stacked against you."

"Do you think I killed Jason Rapp?" asked Oakley.

"It damned well doesn't matter what I think. I'm going to meet with Desmond, give him a piece of my mind, have dinner and return to Orbitus."

"I need you to clear my name."

I took a few steps down the corridor and kept my back to him. "Get yourself a lawyer."

His voice echoed outward. "Come on, Mr. Cobb."

The tightening in my throat was clear enough evidence he didn't kill Rapp, but I knew if I went after the real killer I would become involved in an entanglement leading toward Ariana Cervantes. I marched back to the lattice. "I don't know what I can, as one man, do."

"I fear for my life, Mr. Cobb."

Patenaude gestured as he spoke. "The detention corridors are constantly scanned, but there are people who can get to you."

I looked into Oakley's eyes. "You're afraid they'll kill you because of what you know about IP-5."

"I can't tell you."

"I understand that."

"IP-5's problems only impact the commitment of the crime."

I stroked my chin, stared at Patenaude and then faced Oakley. "I don't work for free, Mr. Oakley."

"I have savings."

I knew my true motivation, besides clearing Oakley, whom I deemed innocent, was delving into my suspicions about Ariana. "I'll see what I can do."

"You need to find Joe Lockheed."

"Where is he?" I asked bluntly.

"I think only Desmond can answer that."

CHAPTER 13

Patenaude commandeered a roverbus to the Turcotte Dome. After we exited Livingston, I was stunned to learn Oakley was so quickly arraigned for the murder of Jason Rapp. Patenaude, his face red from arguing with Kranz, held the zip to his ear and continued the discussion with Richard Merritt, a court magistrate. "Then I will request a warrant to search Oakley's habitat. No, I didn't know that. Thank you." He slowly lowered the zip from his ear and set it on his lap as the roverbus bounced along the Turcotte Road. "Kranz already obtained the warrant. While we were questioning Oakley!"

"Who promoted that idiot? I would have discharged him a hundred times had I constantly worked with him in the bureau. He's a Turcotte drone."

"I hear you. There's nothing I can do about Kranz right now." He gazed out the roverbus' clear silcoplast.

I saw the tinted Turcotte dome, nearly half the size of Livingston. Privately building even a small dome represented wealth and power. The Turcotte ability to utilize the planet's raw resources into a viable export product was unchallenged for seventy-five years. An empire now existed around the inner solar system, with facilities on Phobos and the asteroids, and markets extended directly to earth importers. As anger boiled inside, I studied the smaller connecting maintenance domes. Desmond Turcotte, more than his brother or his father, thought he deserved special treatment, and with a sense of pride, tacitly declared himself beyond everyone else's rules and regulations. When I worked for the bureau we established a Turcotte link to the Divone syndicate, but because of his superb legal representation, we never prosecuted.

"I'm frankly surprised Desmond would allow us in *Emerald City*."

I grinned. "You know he has us out here because of an ulterior motive that has nothing to do with being gracious."

"I can't wait to hear what he has up his sleeve. Maybe he'll produce Joe Lockheed. And he sent Jarred safely away in the Caribbean. I tried getting him, but his zip is off."

"Looks like Desmond has us right where he wants us."

* * * *

The gray Victorian estate's awnings extended down from the upper windows and the sloping porch provided a splendid illusion of a late nineteenth century earth mansion. A perfectly sheared grass lawn spread outward to red stables near distant trees near a white arena fence. I stepped from the roverbus and glanced at Patenaude. "I would almost swear I was on earth."

Three Turcotte servants worked on the porch. Desmond sat casually with Alton Bardsley on white wicker furniture. Two blonde women were at the adjacent table. Patenaude nudged my ribs. "Desmond's wife must be off-planet again."

"Desmond's penchant for beautiful women is well known."

"That's an understatement. The man is a tomcat."

A short man in a red succo quickly scampered down the porch stairs. I recognized his parted hair and twirled mustache.

"Harry Cobb."

"Rudy, still keeping the Turcottes happy?"

"Always," he said, glancing at Patenaude. "Jahn."

"Rudy. What kind of mood is he in?" asked Patenaude.

"Let's just put it this way," he said, shaking our hands.

"Annette is off-planet as of last night."

"I understand," said Patenaude and we started across the grass.

"Jahn, I know I can get you some jafrin. Harry?"

"Bourbon."

"Bourbon it is."

Patenaude raised his bushy white brows. I half smiled as I spoke. "If I'm a guest of the Turcottes, I am going to at least tap his private stock."

"Ah, a plan. We need a plan."

"Renie is supposed to call me. Sadie said he had something. I may need that Bourbon." Desmond and Bardsley both stood as we neared the porch stairs. "Here we go."

"Cobb and Patenaude. Sounds like a law firm, Alton or perhaps a business name," said Desmond.

I stopped on the painted floorboards and glanced at the blonde women ahead. Desmond once had athletic potential, but now his face was flabby. "You're looking fit, Desmond."

"Good living will do that to you, Harry."

"Then what's your secret?" I asked and Bardsley grinned.

"Funny," said Desmond, pointing at me. He watched Rudy bring the jafrin and the Bourbon. "Becoming part of the fast track. Case must be unnerving you."

"You're damned right it's unnerving me." Rudy's eyes opened and he placed the full glass of Bourbon in my hand.

"Do I detect a little hostility?"

"You detect a lot of hostility," I said and moved closer.

"Comes with your territory." Desmond motioned to the shorter, gray haired Bardsley. Bardsley had a perpetual smirk.

"You know my lawyer, Alton Bardsley."

"Desmond, cut the formalities. Without Alton, we might be talking in another place."

Desmond laughed and tilted back his head. "But we're not."

"Jim Oakley was just indicted for Rapp's murder," I said. "But you wouldn't know anything about that, would you, Alton?"

"Working with the courts is my livelihood, Jahn. Oakley looks pretty guilty to me."

I wasn't going to tolerate either Desmond's or Bardsley's theatrics. "Tell me about Ariana Cervantes."

Desmond's smile fell with my broadside comment and he raised his brow. "You ought to be able to answer that question better than I."

"And do you know Samantha Evans?" I asked.

"What the hell are you talking about? Who is she and what does she have to do with anything?"

"More than we all think …" I stepped closer. "Why are you hiding Joe Lockheed?"

His blue eyes moistened. "You're getting more daring in retirement, Harry. I wish I could bring Joe Lockheed out right now so he could clear himself. The whole thing is quite self-evident. That trollop, Kara Oakley, gets taken in by Rapp. Everything gets hot and heavy. Oakley finds out about the affair and comes gunning after Rapp. I'm just sorry it happened on my property."

"I'm sure you are. Oakley wanted to kill Rapp, I'm convinced of that, but I don't think he did it."

"They haven't matched his pinpoint to anything."

"Are you defending Oakley, Alton?"

Bardsley produced a quick annoying chuckle. "Jim Oakley is a Turcotte employee."

I touched the Bourbon to my lips and paused. "I guess that liability has got him indicted."

"Enough of this!" cried Desmond. "Save your verbal prowess for the courtroom, Harry."

"I only have one question: Where is Joe Lockheed?"

"I'm hiding him upstairs," said Desmond and he again threw back his head and laughed.

"And what happened at IP-5?" asked Patenaude.

"Oh, a question from the good inspector."

"You don't have to answer anything," said Bardsley.

"I know that, Alton. I know that. Let me say whatever happened within my company."

"You mean your father's company," I said.

"No mind … I will say we had a technical problem out at IP-5, which has been corrected, and had nothing to do with Rapp's murder."

"It did if your boy, Oakley killed Rapp," said Patenaude.

"Because Mrs. Oakley's knowledge allowed Rapp to blackmail Lockheed."

"You have an overactive imagination," said Desmond.

"Let me add my two cents," I said. "How are we to know Oakley wasn't there to kill Lockheed?"

Bardsley moved closer. "That is the most absurd thing I've ever heard."

"Is it? How do we know Oakley wasn't going to take the fall for the mess up?"

"You're very clever, Mr. Cobb," said Bardsley, pushing his tongue along his cheek. "You presuppose a cover-up and then assign your own lame theories to back it up."

"Nothing would surprise me at this point," I said. "Tell me more about your relationship with Ariana, Desmond. You ever bed her down?"

His double take was worth the trip out to the Turcotte dome. "I can't say the thought hasn't crossed my mind, but the answer is no. You sound like the rejected suitor."

"Are you following me around or just sending that Asian man to keep tabs on me? Or even try to kill me."

"You, sir," said Bardsley, "are pushing your luck."

"Am I?"

"Get out … I have had enough of you, Harry," said Desmond and he pointed across the grounds.

"I'll get out. You can do what the hell you want about IP-5, cover it up, lie about it … I don't care. But God help you if you hired that guy to trail me or worse."

"You can speak plainer than that," said Bardsley.

"Point has been made," I said as my zip sounded. I looked down at the flashing red light. "Can I assume I have secure area or are you going to listen in on my calls?"

"I would assume nothing," said Desmond as he retreated into the house with Bardsley following.

Patenaude peered at me and finished his jafrin. "So much for Turcotte cooperation."

"I don't need his help. I'll get to the bottom of this."

"That was a good point about Oakley. What if he was out there to kill Lockheed instead of Rapp?"

I set down the Bourbon without finishing it. "Having met the alluring Mrs. Oakley, I must say this isn't the first time Jim Oakley confronted the problem of marital infidelity."

"True," said Patenaude as Rudy appeared in the doorway.

"I take it you gentlemen will not be staying for dinner."

"Did he have dinner planned?" I asked.

"Yes, he did," said Rudy.

"Enjoy yourself, Rudy," I said and Patenaude and I started down the stairs. I glanced at my zip. "I'm not answering the call until we're in the roverbus and had cleared the Turcotte Dome."

* * * *

Renie materialized on the roverbus' bumpy window. He was inside a food galley and munched on a hot dog. "Harry, the image is bad."

"We're on the Turcotte connector road to Livingston. I apologize. What have you got?"

"You won't like it, mate."

"I'm already having a lousy day. What is it?"

"Ariana inherited Cauldwell's money. The whole blipping estate."

My mouth opened even though I didn't want it to. "She needed to maintain her lifestyle and apparently knew how to do it." I thought back to the evasive Desmond in the dome. "Renie, I also need to know if she has anything going with Desmond Turcotte. Business or pleasure."

"Will do." He took a few bits of the dog and wiped the mustard off his lips. "Now, Samantha Evans' credit is locked as tight as a drum."

"Are you saying you can't get into it?" I asked.

"Not at all. It just may take some time. I know a trader named Glut who can find the right people to get the information."

"Whatever you have to do."

"Good. Glut will get it. I'll call you as soon as I hear something."

"Thank you, Renie." Patenaude rolled his eyes. "What's the matter, Jahn?"

"I'll pretend I didn't hear that about Glut." He slid along the bench. "But don't you find it odd that she got all his estate?"

"I do ..." My zip flashed. Max's name was on the zip window. "Yes, Max. What have you got?"

"I just picked up your conversation with Renie from the office archive. This high lifestyle is something I wanted to speak to you about. She goes through money like a altered inner system con-trader."

Jody stepped next to him. She spoke in a monotone and her face remained flat. "She has lived in a manner atypical of her annual allotment from Amalgamated Sureties, Conversely—"

"What my unemotional friend here, is saying, Ariana's whooped it in the Aegean, Cote d' Azur."

"Where?" asked Patenaude?"

"The Riviera," I answered.

"Amalgamated Sureties is not fiscally sound," said Jody.

"She's gone through the old man's money," said Max.

"Really?" I was shocked by the apparent turmoil surrounding her. "Is that a motive for murder? And what's the Turcotte connection?"

"I heard you ask Renie that." said Max. "We'll check into it, too."

"Good."

"What's you next move, Harry?"

"Max, I may leave for Platinum City in the morning," I said as Patenaude pointed to the arraignment in his zip window. A charge of murder was read against Oakley and he pleaded not guilty. "But right now, I'm not sure who killed Jason Rapp or better yet, why they killed him."

Chapter 14

All evening I was distracted inside Patenaude's habitat. While his grandchildren played in the far room, I sat with Patenaude and Gwen, and two neighbors, but my thoughts centered on Ariana neatly collecting Samantha Evans' lover's estate like a winner at a roulette wheel. I relished the time I spent with Ariana and found her remarkably charming, seductive and pleasant. Yet, the lavish life she led made her vulnerable because she needed to secure funds to feed her desires. In my dreaming, I had assigned financial need as a motive for murder. But why Rapp?

"Harry," said Gwen.

"I'm sorry," I said and my head snapped back.

"Tell us what your feeling is about building additional domes on the surface."

I raised my brows and assumed a conversational posture.

"Additional domes are a necessity for a booming economy and prosperity for all of us. Plus, there are population concerns on earth."

"That is true," said the neighbor. "But why us?"

"Why not, we've barely touched the surface." My mind replayed a conversation with Oakley two hours ago. He denied any notion to kill Lockheed, but still refused to divulge the IP-5 problem.

"Then you don't mind if Mars becomes like earth?" asked Gwen.

"Heck, they've already started charging droits at the Pathfinder and Viking sights up north," said Patenaude. "It will be just like earth."

"We're nowhere near that."

"I agree with Mr. Cobb to a point," said the neighbor.

Patenaude stood. "Any more jafrin?"

"You've got as taker here," I said.

"I have one jafrin," said Patenaude as he headed toward the kitchen." And one for myself of course."

"Excuse me," I said, smiled and headed behind Patenaude into the next room. "I apologize, Jahn. I can't even think."

Patenaude poured the green jafrin from a pewter hourglass carafe. "You want to leave?"

"You mean for Platinum City?"

"Ya," he said and refilled my own mug. "But what do I say to Ariana? Hey, you murdered Rapp because you're a big spender."

"She has questions to answer. Where exactly was she during the day Rapp was killed? Did she know Evans? When is the last time she saw Evans?"

"Oh, it's all covered. Even if she did it. Where's the proof, Jahnny?"

Patenaude raised his bushy brows and sipped the jafrin. Then he exhaled. "Her arm. We need it examined. We find the scar-we know she wore that t-suit."

"That isn't going to happen ... I'm sure Oakley didn't kill Rapp and I agree with what you said. Rapp was after Lockheed. Damn that Desmond."

Patenaude put his arm around my shoulder. "Harry, let your people do the field work. Relax."

"Maybe you're right." My zip sounded. "So, much for relaxing."

"I'll give you some privacy," said Patenaude.

"No, stay." I opened the channel. "Harry Cobb."

"Harry, this is Renie. I didn't think I'd get you live. I did some digging in Platinum City."

"You have something?" I asked and looked at Patenaude. He sipped more jafrin.

"I do. Ariana likes to fire pulsers."

"What? How do you know this?"

"I checked the pulser firing ranges. For the past few years she has alternated between two ranges and has a class-A firing license."

"I'm out of here."

"What was that, mate?"

"I said, I'm heading back to my hotel room, getting my containments and taking the late shuttle to Orbitus. I can meet you in Platinum City in ten hours."

"Do you want me to talk to Ariana?" asked Renie.

"No, no. Keep digging. I'll talk to her. Believe me I'll talk to her."

* * * *

Forty-five minutes later, I checked out of the Dillon and was on a five-story escalator. My Asian friend, now wearing silver fatigues, appeared on the second floor. He quickly ducked into a side corridor and I pulled out my zip. I was connected to hotel security. I descended to the first floor and onto the shorter escalator. For the next hour, we searched the hotel, but once again, he had slipped away.

I called Desmond from the port terminal and was surprised when he actually took my call. I didn't see Bardsley, but Brandon Turcotte was in Desmond's office. Desmond found my assertions about the Asian man amusing and taunted my impotence in the investigation. I hung up and stepped up to the scanning counter. After I was scanned and on the shuttle ramp, I suddenly suspected Desmond's link to Ariana was more than social.

I took my recliner up front and prepared for sleep once we reached orbit. While I waited for the shuttle's departure, I accessed an old western movie and put on ear covers. I viewed the movie as the shuttle taxied on the port runway. The air whooshed, and with a plethora of noises, we moved into the port surrounds. Once on the main runway and exposed to the outside atmosphere, I glanced up at the stars. Ariana had agreed to meet with me when I first saw her on Orbitus, but only as a diversion to her true intent.

The three internal engines produced a low hum as the shuttle angled up and the horses in the movie crossed a dusty plain on earth. Cowboys hoisted guns into the blue sky as they entered the western town. These men looked mean and the townsfolk cowered along the street's boardwalk. I extended my legs and was pushed into the recliner during the acceleration. Once again my zip sounded.

I rolled my eyes, stopped the movie playback and plugged in my zip. Max and Jody stood in the sunshine on a city sidewalk. "Harry, we have something significant."

"Tell me it involves someone other than Ariana Cervantes."

"Not directly, but Amalgamated Sureties." I fought the acceleration forces. "I see you're leaving the planet. You want us to call back?"

"No, tell me. I don't want to wait."

"Rapp's insurance policy. The recipient is a woman named Angel Vidal. She lives in Platinum City now. I called Renie."

"Good."

"It was sold twenty-five years ago by a guy who worked only a short time for Amalgamated. Name was Mark Lebel, listed as residing here in Baltimore, but we can't find him. At least yet."

* * * *

I never watched the rest of the movie nor could I sleep once the flight smoothed out to Orbitus. In Platinum City, the woman I thought was attracted to me, who may have even contemplated a longer relationship, now topped my list of Jason Rapp's killers. I had trouble with her wishy-washy story of being alone in the Orbitus hotel room the day of the murder. Private transport records, checked by Patenaude, while incomplete, showed no evidence of Ariana or Samantha Evans, making private arrangements for a flight to Livingston. Link Transport, a company subsidized by the Turcotte kondroits, flew regular freight and passenger trips from Orbitus to the Martian surface. My attempts to check the records were halted by flight clerks. So, I called Patenaude. He was interested in the Link angle and would go to court if necessary to obtain a passenger list.

While everyone in the shuttle slept, I worked window connections, using a transcan service to access her name, and attempted to construct a record of her public movements from six years ago at the time of the Evans and Cauldwell deaths. I found accounts of her hosting numerous social events. What garnered my attention was a listing of people attending an event at the Cervantes estate outside the city later in the year, on September 30, 2139. Both Cauldwell and Samantha Evans were listed as invited guests. I crossed the date of her disappearance with the party date. The first report of Evans' disappearance was from her home in Baltimore, only six days after the party.

The window blazed with the report as I leaned back in the recliner. If I accepted my own logic, I would admit Ariana eliminated Evans as a rival to Cauldwell's estate and then absorbed part of Evans' credit control. Yet, no open transactions involving Samantha Evans' credit occurred from October 3, 2139 until the check-in at the Dillon a few days ago. The only reason the Dillon transaction as well as the rover rental occurred because of security procedures requiring a credit payment. I continued my reasoning and concluded Ariana, if she really had access to Evans' credit, befuddled by the new regulations, when arriving on the Mars, on the day of the murder.

My eyes ached. I pinched my nose and thought back to the Barsoom Dome. That time in the jagged mountains near towering falls pouring into the gorge was an idyllic fancy, capped with my obvious idealization of Ariana. Plain facts were always indisputable in the face of bias and strong emotions such as love. I wanted to believe, just as I had the other night in Livingston, of a greater love between the two of us. Yet, she never contacted me, even with my own repeated memos, after we left Barsoom. I just didn't want to believe she was capable of operating within a world outside my own realm. Her list of lovers beguiled sensibility.

I shut off the window and wanted to sleep, but could only keep my stinging eyes closed. Maybe I was dead wrong in my suspicions. A simple alibi on Orbitus would clear Ariana of any complicity in Rapp's murder and a scan of her skin, at the point where cold burn would have set in, would absolve her. The existence of Samantha Evans would also remove Ariana from the suspects. I questioned whether any of those facts could tilt in Ariana's favor, but as we neared Orbitus, I sensed evidence would only accumulate against her.

* * * *

At three in the morning I walked into an Orbitus port restroom. I splashed water and a tingling barsac lotion on my face. The soothing vapors seeped into my sinuses and eyes, negating the fatigue and discomfort. They used to call it jet lag in the old days. Just a plain lack of sleep was enough for me. Most of my containments were aboard the Platinum City flight now fueling above. I picked up my smaller containment, but quickly dropped it and grabbed my pulser when I heard another pulser's charging hiss in the stall ahead. I was tired enough to make the stupid move of racing forward. I kicked open the stall as the disposer sounded and a nimble man in a black leather succo looked into my eyes.

"Who the hell are you?"

"I beg your pardon," he said in a high-pitched voice.

"I heard a pulser charging in here."

"Sir, I don't own a pulser." I stepped back, but kept my pulser trained on him as he exited the stall. His dark eyes darted between the door and the sinks. "Are you a security officer?"

"I am a retired Bureau officer." I showed him my status badge. "I asked you a question, Mister. Who are you?"

He produced a small disk. I inserted it in my zip. "George Kirby. I'm on a flight to visit my daughter in Platinum City."

According to the disk he was telling the truth. Additionally, the scan showed he was employed by Link Transport as a mechanic. "You work for Desmond Turcotte."

"The Turcottes have a controlling interest in Link."

"Really … Do you know Ariana Cervantes?"

"No … Listen, I don't have to be questioned like this."

"You know what the penalty for disposing of a pulser is here on Orbitus?" He just stared at me. "Fifteen years at a level two detention colony. You want to tell me why you are following me?"

"You can call my daughter."

"Maybe I will." I scanned his image into my zip.

"And that is legal?" he asked.

"As legal as I need it to be. You can go, Kirby, and you tell Desmond I'm not dropping this."

He took back his disk, tucked it in his wallet and didn't say anything more as he left the restroom. I followed him out the door and found it interesting he didn't have a bag. Within seconds I memoed the incident to Orbitus and Platinum City security. I added memos to Link and Patenaude, but I wasn't sure whether Kirby had any evil intent. As I headed up the escalator, I also questioned why Desmond would want me dead. Only if he believed I might uncover whatever happened at IP-5, would he take steps to get me out of the way. When I reached Terminal Level One, I took my speculations about Ariana to a higher level. I must have presented a direct threat to her.

Through the silcoplast, I looked at the long, sleek blue ship, bright white in the hebons, and capped by the starry dome. Containments moved up transport conveyers and huge silver food modules were stowed in side compartments. My zip sounded. I squinted. My eyes were tired. I pressed my lips and pushed the button. A memo had just arrived from Max. I had another ten minutes before I boarded. I sat in the first recliner row along the silcoplast, pushed the playback and panned the terminal for Kirby as the memo began. "Harry, I'm assuming you're sleeping. Perhaps a bad assumption. I located in my scans another pinpoint murder from six years ago. This guy, Bill McCann was shot to death on June 19, 2145." Max raised his finger. "He was insured by Amalgamated Sureties. I know that because Mark Lebel was listed as the salesman."

"I found that in the legal transaction library. Policy number 634012987, dated February 1, 2120. Lebel sold him the policy at the Vacation Space Resort. McCann continued to live on Vegas for the next twenty-five years until his death."

Max sneered at Jody and continued. "The pulses were untraceable because the shot was quick and precisely applied to his chest. I remind you of Ariana's proficiency with a pulser. If she were involved with Cauldwell she would have access to his pulser. Harry, we need to find Lebel. I find it hard to believe he sold both

Rapp and McCann policies from Amalgamated Sureties and they were both killed by pinpoint. Enjoy your flight."

"Enjoy my flight. Ha!"

Chapter 15

I slept a full seven hours in a weightless berth aboard ship. Before we docked at Platinum City, I scoured under warming beams and changed my clothes. I stepped into my cabin and with a controller opened the drapes. The silver spiked Platinum City cluster dominated the night sky. My eyes shifted to the center dome, now glowing platinum against space and the terrestrial living area. I shook my head as I buttoned my succo and I conjured up images of the countryside Cervantes estate away from the pointed city buildings.

Confronting Ariana was my problem both personally and professionally. Patenaude's investigation was obfuscated by the Turcottes and possibly even Ariana herself. I would be the only one who had the slightest chance to find the truth. In an hour I was due to meet Renie at the Adriatic Lounge and talk to Angel Vidal, the recipient of Rapp's insurance policy.

My zip memo lights flashed red. I accessed the first memo.

"Harry, this is Max. I just want you to know Burroughs's policy is in the next numerical sequence from McCann. Both men were murdered by pinpoint. I find that very interesting and I thought you'd like to know that."

"I do.. You have a pattern, my friend," I said to the playback.

I hit the button again and Sadie came on the screen. "Hi, Harry. I just heard from Oakley. He says he fears for his life and wants another lawyer. He says he'll put up his habitat as collateral."

I wasn't sure whether Sadie was back in the office. So, I put my finger on the memo pad. "Sadie, this is Harry. Have somebody from Bob Quinn's office defend Oakley. All bills to my office. I'm going to be with Renie at the Adriatic in an hour. Let me know how you make out."

I left the zip and leaned on the sill overlooking the Platinum City's spiked buildings. My investigation was open ended, but I was sure I would need every detail if I were going to confront Ariana directly.

* * * *

The Adriatic's balcony provided a stunning view of the sharp edged, iridescent Platinum dome scrapers, forming a wide canyon overlooking rolling, forested hills into the countryside. The city was so large, clouds, usually thin wisps, formed thousands of meters above the surface.

My zip sounded. "Cobb."

"Harry, it's Renie, turn around." I spun at the rail and saw the sandy haired Renie sitting with a well-preserved woman with light orange short hair and a silky blue costume. Renie smiled. "What do you say, mate?"

I lifted the zip to my mouth as I headed toward the restaurant tables. "I say you're getting billed for this call."

"My pleasure."

I clipped the zip on my belt as Renie stood in his denim succo and extended his hand. "I've been digging."

"Good, what have you got?"

Renie motioned toward the woman. "Harry Cobb, meet Angel Vidal."

Angel stood, revealing more than I wanted to see of her little oval breasts. She was loaded with cheap perfume and spoke with an earth accent, perhaps from New York or New Jersey. "Mr. Cobb, a pleasure I'm sure."

"Call me Harry and please sit down."

Renie ordered drinks. He squinted as he spoke. "Harry, Angel, as I told you, will get 619 droits."

"Excuse me, Angel, do you have your policy number?"

"Sure, I guess I do."

"Can I see it?"

"Ya," she said and placed a woven leather pocketbook onto the table. She dragged out a dozen envelopes, pads, and a fingernail polish canister.

"Let me know if it's 634012989."

She unfolded several papers wrapped in a blue, thicker paper. "That's it. How did you know?"

"Lucky guess," I said and winked at Renie. "Is there a date this policy was sold?"

"February 24, 2120. See, I was there."

"You were?"

"See, I was a dancer on the Neismith. Jason was my … well, my *friend* on that ship. He was in a poker game with—"

"Mark Lebel," I said.

"I ain't got that good a memory from twenty five years ago, but the guy lost big time to Jason. Jason told me later he cheated him out of the policy. Jason put me as the beneficiary of that policy because of my … well for services … performed … if you know what I mean."

"I understand, Miss Vidal. So, you live here in Platinum City now?"

"Yes, sir, Mr. Cobb."

"When's the last time you saw Jason Rapp?"

"Three years ago. He was still … still the same old Jason."

"I bet he was." I looked to Renie. "Renie, let's connect the dates of McCann's and Burroughs's policies."

"We already can place McCann on Vegas and Burroughs on Mars, probably part of Lebel's trail, if it was around the same time period. What do you make of it, Harry?"

"A salesmen making a living. What else do you have?"

"Excuse me, Angel," said Renie. We both stood and walked to the rail. "I think I found a somebody on the Amalgamated payroll. He was checked into the Dillon when you were and the previous night he was in a company habitat on Orbitus. His name is Lo Hui."

"Good work … I'd like to know where he is now and that other guy, Kirby, in the men's room."

"That could be a coincidence."

"You have his image."

"No matches to George Kirby on the general listing. He's like a ghost. I've got people working on other files."

"What about Evans' credit?"

"Glut is supposed to get back to me any time. He'll get to the bottom of it. I heard your memo about Oakley. I believe him. His life isn't worth a plug nickel."

"Bob Quinn will send somebody to Livingston. Can you get any deeper into Amalgamated records?" I asked.

"I doubt it."

"Maybe we need covert activity."

Renie stared at me. "Harry, I'll do whatever you want. Can I say something?"

"Sure …"

"I think your relationship with Ariana is pushing you into area you might want to let the authorities go."

"Nobody will pursue it. And maybe you're right, Renie. Maybe it is personal. As soon as we're done here, I'm going back to my little hotel and then boarding a tram to the Amalgamated Building. If she's not there I take a tracer to the Cervantes estate."

Renie put his hand on my shoulder. "Harry, if she is the killer. She must be ruthless. I don't know why. But somebody so cold hearted isn't going to spare you because of a few days ten years ago at the Barsoom Dome."

"I have to know the truth."

"It's your call, mate. Buzz me if you need me."

"I just may do that."

* * * *

From the vantage point of a small tram station park, the disk shaped Amalgamated Sureties building, dotted with luminous square windows, was set atop a rigid tripod grid within the city's pointed structures. The trams to the city ran every fifteen minutes. I had just learned when I called the main building that Ariana had a late meeting and would not leave for another thirty minutes. I never understood the power Ariana commanded until I gazed at that massive building. Writing policies and insuring large entities had made her father a fortune. For Ariana, with her extravagant lifestyle, to fritter any of the money seemed incomprehensible, and apparently, she had risked the company itself or at least made bad judgment on company investments.

What bothered me, as I paced the bricks, were the three policies, all in numerical order and all connected by pinpoint pulser deaths. I pushed my zip and connected to Renie. At first, he appeared on the darkened zip window, but I quickly moved under the soft orange hebons and plugged into a window ahead. He was still with Angel Vidal and she looked drunk.

"Renie, those three policies. I'm not an insurance guy. What's the big attraction? It isn't like Angel is getting a whole lot of compensation here."

"No, she's not. Maybe we need to look at it from the other end."

"What do you mean?"

"What has Amalgamated got to gain by all this?" asked Renie as Angel put her arm around his ribs.

"On the contrary, they are out, what is it, six hundred and nineteen droits. Come on, that's a few nights on the town."

"I'm sure Angel doesn't mind."

"I don't mind," she said, slurring her words.

Renie removed her arm and leaned toward the window.

"Harry, insurance companies make their money by predicting the odds of loss and investing the money to cover that loss at the best rate."

"Sure, I understand that, but what ... how the hell do these policies reflect what you're saying?"

"I don't know and don't know what they would do with money taken in by this guy Lebel."

I stared at the Amalgamated Building. "That's the key, what is their return on the policies?"

"I need more records and they're as tight as ..." He paused as Angel kissed his neck. "They're tight. We may have to just figure this thing out on our own."

"What *is* their return?" I asked and heard the city tram approach. The first car appeared in the late afternoon light around the tree-lined bend. "I have to go, Renie. Solve my problem."

"I'll give it my best shot. Do me a favor, Harry."

"What's that?"

"Check in with me every six hours. I don't trust her."

"Agreed on both counts."

I unplugged the zip and hurried back to the platform. The levitated tram approached along the concave track, rocking gently and slowed. I entered a nearly empty car as the doors opened vertically. I sat back in the soft recliner with my back to the building and I thought about Renie's warnings. Reasoning directed me away from confronting Ariana, but pride and a natural curiosity stirred as the tram pulled from the station.

I moved away from this isolated portion of the city and when the forest ended, a slew of habitat buildings rose from the ground. Slowly, I tapped my fingers on the armrest and wished I knew more about the insurance business, but I was certain Renie, with his street-wise savvy, would translate any details about the three policies.

I noticed my zip was flashing and touched my index finger on the pad. With my eyes closed I listened to an audio memo from Patenaude, left forty-five minutes ago.

"Harry, I hope this memo finds you well. FYI: Oakley and Lockheed. Out of thin Martian air our good friend Mr. Lockheed has popped up at Oakley's pretrial hearing. He has testified under oath, and I have all the testimony if you want it memoed, that Oakley killed Rapp."

"No, no, no," I said and looked around the car.

"I first must say I don't believe a word of it and Robert Quinn's associate, Damon James, really put the screws to him, asking why he didn't come out with this days ago. He asked Lockheed why and where he was hiding. Apparently, he was at IP-7 the whole time, which to me is unconscionable on Desmond's part. Here's my take on it: I think Lockheed is saying exactly what the Turcottes want him to say in order to take Desmond out of the picture because of this IP-5 thing.

We found from our subpoenaed plant records that Desmond, Oakley and Lockheed met eleven times over the past two weeks. I know you're pursuing the Ariana leads and I will talk to you directly, but I wonder if Desmond may have ordered both Lockheed and Oakley to kill Rapp. Oakley got him first."

"No, Jahn. No."

"When James cross-examined both men about IP-5's problems, Alton Bardsley objected, claiming IP-5's potential problems had nothing to do with the Rapp murder."

"Maybe," I said to my zip and glanced up at the Amalgamated Building hovering close as I neared the heart of the city.

Patenaude continued. "Judge overruled, but neither men would talk about it. Desmond sat there smug with a smirk on his face that I would have liked to have wiped off with a left hook to the jaw."

Another memo flashed. I paused Patenaude's memo. Renie was at the railing, overlooking the city. "Yes, Renie."

"Harry, Glut has nothing on Evans at this time, but he's close. What he did find is Amalgamated is serious trouble. More than we thought. She owes Platinum City back taxes on the Cervantes estate. Glut thinks the whole company could easily go down." A fearful twinge swept my stomach. "And I just talked with Jody. She and Max are gathering information on *another* pinpoint death related to an Amalgamated policy." As he spoke a live memo flashed. "I'll get back to you."

The tram slowed at a platform directly under the Amalgamated building tower. Max's image was not clear until I fully exited the tram. "Max, Renie says you've found another policy."

"This is getting very interesting. A guy named Hal Anderson. Worked in the Turcotte owned Link Transport on Orbitus. Killed by a pinpoint to the head. A precise hit. Anderson was killed the day before Billy McCann at the Vegas Colony and his policy number end ends in eight-six, in direct numerical connection to McCann, Burroughs and Rapp. It was a ridiculous policy only worth two-hundred and fifty-nine droits upon death."

"What's going on, Max?"

"May I speculate, Harry?" asked Jody.

"Please do."

"If we extrapolate the mean value of the existing policies and the projected rising investment acceleration, the resulting allocation of funds would be a direct ratio of the first investment."

"What the hell does that mean?" asked Max. "Talk English for Pringle's sake, will you? What I have to put up with ..."

"What are you saying, Jody?" I asked as I looked directly upward through the metal grids toward the building disk hundreds of meters above me.

"A poor investment of funds in favor of the policy holders could produce a windfall over time."

"Are you saying any of these policy holders could cash in the policies?" I asked.

"That is what she means," said Max. "The longer they live, the more valuable the policy becomes. And, Harry, we found Mark Lebel, but not in good shape."

"What does Lebel say?"

"Not much, he's in a rehab facility with brain degeneration. He's undergoing revigoration therapy, but right now he can't speak right now. We're asking yes and no questions, but he tires very easily."

I again looked to the shadowed underbelly of the Amalgamated disk. "So, we have president of the company killing policy holders. Why not one of her people? Like Lo Hui. I'm convinced he tried to kill me."

"I don't know about that," said Max, pressing his lips.

"I'm just wondering how many of these policies Lebel sold."

"Where was the Anderson policy sold?"

"Oh ... on the Neismith."

"Seems he took a trip to Mars twenty-five years ago and sold policies along the way." I trod toward the central elevator. "What does this have to do with Desmond's ore problems?"

"Maybe nothing."

"Have Renie check Link Transport. That would be a convenient way to leave Orbitus, travel to Rapp, kill him and get back before the actual shuttle flight back to Mars. That would link Desmond and, as much as he is unscrupulous in business, I don't peg him as a killer."

"Nor do I."

"Perhaps, they shared a commonality related to social interactions and a possibly minor business transactions."

Max tightened his eyes. "I never thought I'd say this, but I agree with Jody."

"This could be a moment of historic proportions." I smiled and entered the clear silcoplast elevator.

"Harry, are you still planning to meet with Ariana?"

"I am unannounced and about to be transported to the top of the Amalgamated disk."

"Be careful. If she's the killer, and you just mentioned somebody else could have carried out these killings, she must *enjoy* killing."

That statement sent a chill throughout my body. The car rose into the grid tower and soon provided a view of the rolling countryside toward the Cervantes estate. "I have other issues, Max."

"I understand."

"What does he mean?" asked Jody. "I thought we discussed in great detail, all the issues."

"I'll explain," he said, rolling his eyes. "Good luck, Harry."

"Thank you." I cut the zip and leaned my head against the wall as the car moved above Platinum City. What again concerned me was Max's thought about Ariana having a predilection for murder. My mind retreated to Barsoom Dome ten years ago. I had once fallen in love with Ariana and she left me. As the elevator raced past silcoplast transparencies of halls and offices, I realized I could easily fall for her again. Lebel sold the policies twenty-five years ago and somebody was slowly eliminating the policy holders. Were there any more policy holders and were they targeted by Amalgamated or Ariana? I unclipped my zip and sent a memo to Patenaude. "Jahn, I am finding Amalgamated policy holders, killed in numerical sequence of policy. Amalgamated is in serious financial trouble and so is Ariana. And, one more for the road: A dead policy holder, Hal Anderson, worked for Desmond's Link Transport. I'm wondering if that's how Rapp's killer got to Mars. Put that in your jafrin ..." I attached the policy information. "I'm going to talk with Ariana. Keep me briefed on Lockheed and Oakley."

The car slowed and the doors opened to a spacious main lobby with a glossy floor and a silcoplast span above Platinum City. I hesitated and wasn't sure whether to drop the whole investigation. I was hired by no one now and had no vested interest in Oakley's freedom. Still, I walked forward toward the window marquee. I had to confront her.

Chapter 16

I thought about posting a memo on the marquee board, but I was dissuaded by a creeping inner fear that I was dealing with someone who could kill with a skewed inner justification. A building schematic, obtained by repeated attempts through my zip and the original city records, clearly showed a tracer strip and craft preparations adjacent to a support elevator on the eightieth floor of the disk. Additional scans still placed Ariana within the building.

I entered the elevator and figured I might run into security problems by heading to the tracer strip. As I rose through the disk I reminded myself Amalgamated was a business building and not a military or security enclave, but I was sure window scanners would surely follow my progress.

Once on the eightieth floor I stepped into an open lobby, so high I felt I was near the clouds back on earth. At a sunken reception area, several woman answered zip calls on rounded windows. I shuffled forward, gazing down a straight metal corridor, rising into a wide set of white stairs. I knew from the schematics, the tracer strip entry was located at the top of the stairs. One of the women asked if I needed help and I told her I had to assemble my memos. She was busy at the desk, nodded and answered another zip. I sat along the silcoplast span, activated my own zip and specifically reviewed public records.

An investment house analysis advocated an overhaul of all aspects of the company and a rewriting of policies to increase immediate revenues at the expense of long-term dividend payment. The writer of the report indicated higher premiums and the proper investment portfolio would supersede any long-term higher dividends. As I stood and started down the perforated metal corridor I wondered about Lebel's sale of the original policies to the murdered policy holders.

I checked over my shoulder when I reached a brighter area surrounded by a translucent geodesic dome. Apparently, Amalgamated made its money by charging premiums which were invested the funds to bring profits. I studied my zip window as I started up the stairs. Yielding a profit from the premiums allowed the companies to pay death benefits down the line, but I noticed in the report, some policies were not just death benefits policies. After many years of paying premiums certain holders could treat the policy as a personal investment.

I passed a few people on the stairs and stepped onto the upper level corridor, open to the best panorama I had seen of the city and countryside. To my left was the gray tracer strip and a luxurious red and blue company tracer with the gold company letters emblazoned across the body and the steamy ejection on the side vents indicated the pending departure. I stood at the span and finalized my thoughts about the policies.

I didn't have proof, but was thinking Lebel sold policies, yielding tremendous personal dividends over time. Given the shaky financial condition of Amalgamated Sureties, a large number of policies, each coming due at an inopportune time, would severely crunch the company funds if the original premiums were not invested correctly. A death benefit would only require the face value of the policy.

I remained pensive as I descended a metal framed side stairway. A good prosecutor could easily have staff scrutinize the policies. With simple ledger accounting, the discrepancy of the murdered policy holders versus the company savings would align with the eliminated clients. I still could not accept, as I wandered along a lower corridor paralleling the large tracer, Ariana as the killer. She had the means, with subordinates like Lo Hui, to have the murders carried out systematically in different places and quietly pay the death benefits.

An outside elevator extended to offices up the disk facade. At the connecting corridor to the tracer strip I was now sure Ariana was the killer, but desperately wanted evidence to the contrary. For an executive of a company to personally engage in such an operation meant something I did not want to admit. Such a person would enjoy the hunt, the kill and the result. This was especially true if she left Orbitus, possibly via Link Transport, and tracked down Rapp like an animal on the run. To return to Orbitus and subtlety arrive on her original shuttle flight required a certain moxie I respected on some surrealistic level.

I heard movement on the staircase above. Ariana wore a shapely pink succo, open to the shoulders, and she glided with several aides in gray succos, in a moving business conference. The discussion abruptly ended when she spotted me below. I made it my business to watch every body movement, each change in her facial muscles, and the intensity and alignment of her eyes. She said something to her aides and they looked at me as they retreated up the stairs. My heart slammed against my ribs as her pink velvet lips parted and she moved her torso down the stairs.

Was I watching the approach of a mass killer or an individual who orchestrated mass murder? I found her dark eyes alluring enough to wish I hadn't put myself in this position. Maybe my reasoning about the polices was only a concocted story, an erroneous conclusion to get her out of my life. She extended her hand, fingers displaying rings with assorted colorful gems, and her perfume was sweet. "Harry, what are you doing here?"

I don't know why I kissed her hand nor do I know why I said what I said. "I had to see you again."

She smiled perfunctorily this time. "I understand what's going on here."

"You do?"

She wrapped her arm around my arm and brought me down the corridor toward the awaiting tracer. "Of course, you have two reasons to be here. Your investigation has led you here because of Henry Cauldwell, Samantha Evans, and bogus policies sold by Mark Lebel."

"That's pretty good."

Her hand was warm and her silken succo rubbed against me.

"Additionally, I left our relationship in the lurch on Mars. I'm sorry," she said and stopped. She held my hands at the outside entrance and looked into my eyes. Her scent threatened to overwhelm me and I was uneasy with my intense feelings for her. "I owe you personal and professional explanations."

"You are … a very perceptive woman."

She ran her finger along my lips. "I have to be. Listen, maybe we can have dinner."

"I don't know if that's a good idea," I said.

"Oh, no. You're coming with me."

"Where?"

"To the estate …" Tears formed in her eyes. "Harry, I never should have left you alone in the Barsoom Dome. I'm so sorry."

"Barsoom was an idyllic time." I could feel myself slipping into her grasp and I didn't want to fight it.

"We can relive those days … I'm thinking of selling my company." Again she held out her hand. "Come with me."

I wanted her and what was left of my reason, was diminished to an almost inaudible voice in my head cautioning me to stay away. Her eyes beckoned and I threw away every remnant of sensibility away and took her hand onto the tracer strip. I rationalized illusions of my own invincibility. We climbed the tracer stairs and prepared to travel to the country.

* * * *

The tracer tilted and swung gracefully around the building as Ariana returned with two snifters. "Harry, you know I consider this whole thing my fault. Several of our policy holders have been killed, as you well know, by pinpoint pulser. My mission on Mars was to talk with Lo Hui to—"

"Then he's your man."

She sat across from me at the table and produced a smile that captured a plethora of emotions I didn't understand. "If you mean is he employed by me. Yes, he is. And I sent him to follow you."

"My room was blown apart and I was supposed to be in it!"

Her face seemed stuck in the previous emotion. "Oh, no, Harry, please don't even think what you're thinking. I can say that Lo was aware of what happened and reported back to me immediately."

"I didn't see you running over there." The tracer lifted above the city."

"I knew you were safe."

I was sick of perfect answers and well-timed statements.

"Your company is in financial trouble and so are you."

I had never seen her brow crease so deep. She held my wrist. "Oh, no. No, we're reorganizing.."

"Don't insult me, Ariana. Things are so shaky Amalgamated could fold and your personal spending habits are nothing short of extravagant."

"I admit I have always been on a high social track. I will maintain that track. What I didn't need was any controversy because of these murders."

I nearly exploded with wild emotion. "Then would you mind telling me up front why these people are being killed?"

"We are checking people within the company."

"Isn't it true that these policies, if carried to fruition, would escalate in dividends and ruin your company several years down the line?"

"Ruin? How long have you been in the insurance business?"

"I don't need to be in the insurance business to—"

"If there was such a problem, don't you think I would send in negotiating teams or do it myself?"

She was making a good point. My retort was not verbal. If she was the killer then she liked killing and enjoyed solving her problems with a pinpoint pulser. I wondered, as we left the city limits and whipped over the trees below, why I had allowed myself to come out here at all. "I'm not the only one looking into this. The authorities have questions."

"Let them question. I have lawyers and alibis."

"Do you?" I asked as I stood. "Where were you specifically when Jason Rapp was murdered or any time during that day. Just give me one witness or one written transaction."

Her face soured, but I wasn't sure why. "I had lunch with Lo Hui—"

"Lo Hui," I said and threw back my head in laughter.

"At the Melba Terrace on Orbitus while Jason Rapp was being murdered."

"Were you scanned?"

"I don't know, you'll have to check."

"Where is the credit?" I asked.

"Lo paid for the meal. I'm sure your people can easily access that."

"Then who killed Rapp?"

"How am I supposed to know that?"

I looked at the Cervantes estate, built in tiers on the lush, distant hill. "Don't tell me you don't know Samantha Evans."

"My you are thorough, I'll give you that." She shook her head and her dark eyes moistened. "Samantha was unstable and she wanted Henry Cauldwell. So did I. I won. She lost and disappeared."

"Or was murdered."

"I suppose you're going to nail me on that, too."

"The thought crossed my mind. You have Cauldwell's pinpoint and his entire estate."

"I never had access to any of Henry's weapons."

Now my face was solid. "Really … You spend considerable time at a pulser firing range."

"True … You are good at what you do, Mr. Cobb."

"I have a good team working with me."

"You can forget about me firing a pinpoint owned by Henry Cauldwell. All of the Cauldwell estate was audited by my vice president, Stanley Miller."

I shook my head and exhaled slowly and loudly. "One simple question: Where is Samantha Evans?"

"I assume she is dead because my attempts to locate her have proved fruitless."

"Why would you try and find her?"

"To explain why I was in love with Henry."

"Who else were you in love with?" I asked, biting my lower lip.

She raised her brows and with a cunning smiled answered me. "Oh, love is not love … which alters when it alteration finds."

"Or bends with remover to remove—Sonnet 116. I can quote Shakespeare, too, Ariana. But I have my doubts your professed love to Cauldwell."

"I liked him, I respected him and I took his estate. I'll admit that to you and nobody else, but I had nothing to do with Samantha's disappearance."

"Then where is she?"

"One possibility is she killed herself because to her own misfortune. I think in her own demented way she was in love with Henry."

I wanted to call Ariana a viper, but I didn't, and I found something wild about her deliberate flair. The wide linear wings of the Cervantes estate were visible in the forested hills and I had no business being out here. I would gain nothing by questioning her because she had an answer for everything. The tracer decelerated toward a clearing within the trees out back. As we descended vertically I knew I should stay inside the tracer and return to Platinum City. "Listen Ariana. I think this has gone as far as it should."

She slowly stood and moved closer toward me. The perfume was heavy, yet intriguing. "I do want you to stay for dinner."

"Listen—"

"You have thoughts about me that just aren't true, Harry."

"Where is Samantha Evans?"

Ariana shrugged her shoulders. "Maybe she knew she had lost Henry and she dropped out of sight because she was humiliated."

"Okay, she drops out and never surfaces until her credit is used at the rover rental place."

Ariana slowly nodded we nudged the ground. She took my arm and led me out the side door and onto a sunlit fieldstone terrace. "There was a lens found."

"You're damned right there was a blue lens found and blonde hair!"

"Don't blame me. I didn't use her identity and I know that's what you're saying."

"Then who did?"

Ariana's eyes flared. "You didn't even know Samantha. She had coping problems."

I studied the terraces toward the first tier of the building.

"Then fill me in."

"She was vindictive and plotting. She used Henry and his money. I'm not sorry he gave me everything he had."

"Was he murdered?" I asked.

"I never checked it, but the thought crossed my mind. Look, I wouldn't put it past Samantha even try to frame me. Maybe she had access to company policies. She would have done anything for revenge."

"What about his pulser?"

"There may have been more than one."

I shook my head as I paced the stones. Accepting Samantha Evans herself as the killer would require knowledge of Lebel's policies. "Using her own credit was stupid."

"Maybe she had to."

"You asking me to believe she murdered these people just to hang you?"

"I don't know. I just don't have any other explanation. Harry, you mentioned other people being killed. I can tell you where I was and who I was with."

"You mean just like when Rapp was killed?"

"That's the exception." Ariana's lip curled. "Damn, her. She's the only one who would go to these ends."

I pressed my lips and gazed through the hanging tree branches to the glowing city far away. The tracer hummed, ready to leave, and I was not aboard. My mind clouded and I was unable to form a precise theory. Like someone physically incapacitated I was immovable and speechless as the tracer rose behind me into the dome. A cold chill descended my over skin when I felt her hands on my shoulders. "Ariana, I don't know whether this is smart."

She spoke in a whisper. "I have my staff preparing a quiet dinner. Let's go inside and collect our thoughts."

I furrowed my brow and turned. Her eyes captivated me again and I didn't like it. "All right."

Chapter 17

Her power attracted me, her charms seduced me, but her story baffled me. I immediate memoed my people and wanted to hear other explanations about a possible Samantha Evans revenge and cover up. In my suite I stepped into a warm, bubbling surge of water and fragrance, filling an elevated, tiled tub overlooking a spectacular garden and luminous pool highlighted by colored hebons. Later, relaxed and dressed in a casual succo, I checked my zip before heading down to the drawing room. I found it odd no one had called me and checked my zip transmission records. My attempts to send memos at the terrace were thwarted by an overhead scanning system that allowed only confirmed passwords. I was upset with myself for not having left the estate earlier. Despite Ariana's hospitality I now wanted to request transportation back to Platinum City where I could transmit my memos.

I stepped into the hall and moved to the open elevator, overlooking a voluminous circular room with a huge, glossy white table and high back chairs. Servants buzzed about side tables filled with enough food to feed a dozen people. Center tapered pale green candles flickered in the breeze. The open span faced Platinum City, now a dim patch beyond the hills and trees.

When I reached the lower level two servants in beige succos, trimmed with red silk, approached me. "Mr. Cobb, Miss Cervantes will arrive momentarily."

"I was going to ask her if—"

"Miss Cervantes requests you be seated."

I did not want to be ungracious, but wanted to contact the outside. Maybe it was best I talked to Ariana directly. "Very well."

They escorted me to the chair. A waiter appeared and poured water from a moisture beaded metal pitcher. I stared the linen wrapped green glass champagne bottle. The night air tickled my neck and arms, and I was mesmerized by the moving candle flames.

"Harry …"

Through the dancing flames she appeared in a light blue ruffled dress, bare at the shoulders and white gloves. Her hair was now woven upward with wisps along her smooth white neck, her lips outlined in a subtle red rouge and eyes highlighted a smooth azure shade. I stood and her image crystallized in the orange light. "You look … *radiant*."

"Thank you."

I moved around the table and pulled back her chair before the servant could arrive. She wore a new, pervasive perfume. I looked down the nape of her neck and placed my hands on her delicate shoulders. She raised her hand and I kissed the smooth glove. "How could I leave such a presence?"

"I'm glad you traveled to Platinum City."

"I seem to be in the middle of conflicting interests," I said and returned to my chair. "You make a persuasive argument implicating Samantha Evans."

"It is not my intention to blame Samantha for anything. I can only tell you the truth.. My people are trying to track her down. I have Stanley arriving for dessert. He can explain more about Mark Lebel and the polices. Or so he says … But let's not talk about that now. Let's talk about us."

I was leery. "Okay."

"Barsoom was a time I wished could have gone on forever." She looked down and then brought the water glass to her lips. Her eyes were distant over the rim. "I was afraid of just how close I was getting to you. *Scared* … I left because I could see where it was going."

"And where was that?"

"I would have gone anywhere you wanted to go." I stared into her dark eyes, but realized I was grinding my teeth. "I never experienced a time where I lost myself."

"Why didn't you tell me that?" I asked.

"You never admit things you're running from, especially to the one you're running from."

"No, I suppose not. But it's always stuck in my side and been something I never got over. And now I feel as if I'm being led down the same road."

She looked devotedly into my eyes. I was taken aback within the mix of emotions, including the distinct possibility everything she told me now was designed to divert me from confronting her not only Rapp's killer, but a ruthless provocateur of death, who protected her precious standard of living. Again, she spoke in almost a whisper. "Harry, I would have never asked you to join me in Livingston when you walked up to my table outside the gambling hall unless I wanted to be with you."

I didn't know that, but I wanted to believe it. I desperately wished to rectify the pain I felt after Barsoom ten years ago. The army of servants that descended on the table delivered a seven-course feast lasting nearly two hours. After my initial reservations, Ariana, the astute social player, altered her amorous line of attack, and shifted to a splendid conversational mode. I lost track of the case.

* * * *

We had just finished a curious blend of ice cream, apple glaze, and pudding when, almost on cue, a tall serious man with receding, stringy red, peppered hair, stepped into the room. He wore a gray, matted succo and carried a small containment. Ariana seemed aware of his presence before she saw him. "Harry, this is Stanley Miller. He was with my father for fifteen years and has helped me through the transition."

Miller's shifting eyes bothered me from the start and his constricted sentences and high-pitched voice made me think he had no personality. "I understand you have concerns about policies sold by Mark Lebel twenty-five years ago."

I wasn't sure how to approach this guy. "Yes, that's true."

"If you will excuse me, I will join you momentarily, Harry," said Ariana.

I stood and watched her leave the room through a small paneled door near the open window span. Then I faced Miller. He propped his containment on the table where I had just enjoyed a wonderful meal and delightful conversation. He activated the window on the upper side of the containment. "Mark Lebel only worked for Mr. Cervantes for a short time. He recklessly sold policies on a trip from earth to Mars."

"Why the hell are you telling me this?" I wondered what Ariana was up to and why Miller had a dumbfounded look on his smooth face. "Well?"

"Miss Cervantes expressed a concern."

"Did she?" I asked.

"Yes, she was afraid and I concur you are drawing erroneous conclusions about these policies."

"Really?"

"Yes." He moved something on the window. I saw a copy of McCann's policy. "These policies have no value to us. Certainly, paying a death benefit after twenty-five years of investment—"

"Stop right there, Mr. Miller. I'm not an insurance guru, but I damned well know of policies where the policy holder can cash in the invested value of the policy years later."

"That is true of course, but not the case here." He was too sure of himself. "You can check all the numbers and where we invested the money. Our ratio of profitability is quite good. The bottom line is Amalgamated Sureties has no vested interest in these people being killed. I think we are looking at mere coincidence."

I decided to take a different tact and acknowledge Samantha Evans was alive and trying to frame Ariana. "But a novice in the industry might misinterpret the structure of the policy and indeed think your company would lose a great deal of money. Especially if Mr. Lebel was selling out on the limb with promises of fantastic returns to the purchaser."

"Oh, Mr. Cervantes never would have allowed that." Miller flashed a lip smile lasting less than a second. "You never met him, did you?"

"As a matter of fact I did and I know he was a busy man." I had a strong sense Miller or one of his subordinates could have easily doctored these policies. Such changes would not stand up in a court of law and was confabulated only to deceive me. "I'd like to look at the original codes and dates on the imputed policies."

"I am not a computer expert, Mr. Cobb."

"Then get one."

"If you are implying documents have been altered—"

I stood and moved up to him. "I'm a private investigator, Mr. Miller. Like you and your capacity, in my own way I require an accounting for everything. Everything."

"We believe Samantha Evans misinterpreted the policies and has been on a killing rampage because she lost Henry Caul-dwell to Miss Cervantes."

"You parroted that one very well," I said, glancing at the colorful graphics on his window.

"I don't know if I like you insinuations," said Miller, but he did not close the containment. "I will get you those codes."

"No, Mr. Miller, you'll get the codes for the courts. What you can get me is a working zip. All communications are blocked out here and I don't like it."

"I have nothing to do with communication."

"So, I see."

"You are very insulting, Mr. Cobb," he said, deactivating the window and he closed the containment. "Good evening."

"That remains to be seen."

Again he produced the annoying, instant lip smile and walked briskly toward the stairs. He was gone quickly and I was alone in the spacious room. I had no weapon and no means to reach my office or anyone else. Perhaps I should have remained passive and not challenged Miller. By directly confronting what he was saying I may harve set in motion a chain of events to threaten my own well-being.

* * * *

For the next fifteen minutes I badgered the servants. At first I was pleasant, but I grew anxious when no one could find Ariana. I then asked for a zip to talk to my office, but each servant told me such contact required authorization from Ariana. I stared at the light from Platinum City, luminescent in the distant sky. The table behind me was cleared and the candles extinguished, but my anger sizzled with each passing minute. They had assaulted me on two fronts. With Miller's inept presentation I was more convinced Samantha Evans was dead because Ariana needed her dead, just as she needed the policy holders dead. While I was not sure how many more policy holders lurked on the horizon, I was now in her way.

She had tried the seductive approach, which she should have continued. Despite all my speculations about her murdering rampage I fought the realization I still found her alluring and charming. Had she not sent in Miller she could have easily lured me upstairs. Maybe that was still possible, but now my only concern was getting off the estate. Her killing me, someone who was directly challenging her killing scam, was simple: Bring me to the bedroom and murder me. At least I now fought the carnal sensations with an overriding quest for survival.

"How do I get the tracer back here?" I shouted.

"The tracer remains berthed at the company building," said the servant near the door.

"Then kindly requgest the transportation for me. I will pay for it. I wish to leave at once."

"Miss Cervantes has not authorized—"

I walked across then parquet floor. "I really don't give a damn what she has or hasn't authorized, I'm leaving … *now*."

"Sir …"

"Okay, then let me call my office. Where is my zip?"

"I'm sorry."

"So am I, Mister, so am I." I stormed down the hall to the outside terrace opening.

"Where are you going?" he asked from behind.

"To Platinum City. I'll walk if I have to."

"It's fifteen kilometers."

"Good, I could stand to shed a few pounds."

I crossed onto the terrace and gazed across the multi-winged estate's stone facade. A few dull yellow hebons blazed along the upper levels. I chided myself for being so stupid. She had no designs on me and I should have known that in the Orbitus gambling hall. Ten years ago she wanted a fling in Barsoom Dome and then resumed her fast track life. I didn't like being played for a sucker.

I marched down the fieldstone stairway, along green hebons outlining the tropical plants. At the lower level, between the surrounding forested hills, the gardens ended, but a small path cut into denser underbrush. On the path I only saw the upper dome's glow and with each step along the dirt, I constantly looked over my shoulder. I was unarmed and had no means to communicate. Nor did I like the fact they had my zip.

A clear unrecognizable voice shot out of the bushes to my right. "You will come out of the bushes."

"Identify yourself."

"I am in charge of security for the estate. Come out now!"

I saw a gray image of the estate back over the hill and panned the thick fauna around me. "So, she couldn't do it herself, could she?"

"I do not know what you are talking about."

"My guess is you have a pulser pointed at my head."

He laughed, I dove on my belly into the bushes, and the red flash from a pulser beam lit the immediate area above me. I crawled on my stomach through the leaves and branches as the beam swung wildly, cutting trees and bushes within centimeters of my head. As branches flayed against my cheeks, I made headway from the beam, but fires broke out in the dry leaves behind me.

The shooting stopped, but I continued like a scampering rat through the brush. I had lost direction and kept moving. The reflection of flames crept onto the upper trees. Those fires and my quick dive into the bushes had spared my life.

* * * *

For the next hour as small overhead sprayers doused the fires, I followed the base of the hill and finally climbed to a ledge with a good view of Platinum City. The Amalgamated disk rose above the other buildings and a spread of suburban lights twinkled across the valley.

I turned back to the estate. The fires were long since out, but I took nothing for granted. Ariana was not going to just let me skip into Platinum City with the knowledge she had ordered my death and she was aware of my cognizance of her game with the policies. I started down a dirt embankment, but heard a small tracer in the air behind me. With my hands placed along the smooth edges I moved sideways on the hill. A spotlight shined down from the approaching tracer.

I started up the hill and as I gained elevation I heard the same voice from back in the clearing. He taunted and cursed me by name, and fired the pulser into the fauna below. I grabbed onto rock edges and tree roots as I hoisted myself upward. The valley and Platinum City were spread before me, but at the top I peered straight down the ledge.

Several red beams split the rocks around me. I backed into an indented scarp, but was trapped between the rocks and the tracer. Three men in gray fatigues fired again, the upper rocks chipped and showered me with debris as another tracer moved up from the valley. I heard loud voices. Then the pulser beams ceased, the little tracer slowly backed away, but the other craft brushed the cliff.

Ariana, in red fatigues and matching realball cap, wielded a pinpoint inside the opening. She walked onto the rock surface and I deliberately moved toward her. "Decided to come in for the kill yourself, eh, Ariana?"

"I'm glad I reached you. My security detail were only doing their job to protect the estate from intruders."

"Go ahead, kill me. Get over with …"

"You think I'm here to kill you?"

I produced a gallows laugh. "Oh, Ya."

She glanced at her pinpoint and tucked in a side holster.

"Oh, no. Harry, Stanley just received the news. I want you to come back to the estate."

"What news?"

"Lo Hui has been arrested by Inspector Patenaude."

"What?"

"He has a record of killing I was unaware of. Patenaude is convinced he killed Jason Rapp and the others."

I didn't believe her, but she did have the pulser. "Okay, bring me back and let me call Patenaude and anyone else I want to."

"Of course."

"Really? Where the hell is my zip and why are all communications shielded?" I stepped only a few meters away from her.

"I think you have the wrong impression of what's going on here."

"What am I supposed to think? My zip is gone and everything else is blocked."

"Purely a security precaution."

I studied her compact body in the fatigues and thought back to the designs I had on her at dinner. "Let me call Patenaude right now."

She stared at me and then turned toward the tracer. "Get me a zip."

I wondered if Lo Hui was only implementing her directives. That theory made more sense than anything advanced thus far. Somebody handed her a small zip from inside and she held it out.

"Here."

I felt the edges of her smooth hand as I retrieved the zip and immediately opened a connection to Patenaude in Livingston. Visual was nonexistent, but Patenaude's familiar cadence reverberated over the zip. "Where are you, Harry? We've been trying to reach you for hours."

"Not important right now, Jahn. Tell me what you know."

"A confession from your shadow, Lo Hui. He works for Ariana." My eyes caught Ariana's deep eyes. Then I looked back at the zip. "We have records of him being booked on a commercial shuttle flight from Orbitus two days before you arrived."

"What does he say?"

"He says he will funnel all answers through Alton Bardsley."

"Bardsley? Why Bardsley?" I asked, now sensing a Desmond connection.

"I don't know. Bardsley himself was over here. Oakley was released to his own personal recognizance three hours ago." I said nothing but was sure Ariana was linked to the machinations in IP-5. "What exactly did he say?"

"He arrived and admitted having access to Samantha Evans' credit. He used her identity with a facial squeeze, the hair and lens to rent the rover. Before the storm cleared he went back to Livingston. He has a healing cold burn on his right forearm. We've got our man. I only wonder if he killed all the others."

"I think you should check merchantiles in Livingston to see who purchased the facial stuff, the wig and lens."

"Lo did. We have records."

"You do?" I asked.

"It's all over, Harry. He did it."

Ariana smiled graciously and raised her dark brows. I held the zip as Patenaude continued. "I'm sorry, Ariana."

"I understand why you would think what you did."

"I never suspected Lo Hui in the murders. What is the link to Desmond Turcotte?"

She shook her head. "I don't know. Lo works for me, but I don't account for his every minute. Obviously, something is going on here."

"Yes, you are very right about that."

Chapter 18

She persuaded me to stay in the guest quarters above the glowing blue pool, bordered in white tiles and nestled within thick tropical, leafy plants. More colored hebons spotlighted the pathway back to the main estate. I wasn't sure why I stayed on the grounds, but I didn't discount having guilt about blaming Ariana for the murders, or perhaps I longed for the evening's excitement anticipated at dinner. More likely I was extremely confused about everything.

I sipped on a cool fruit nectar late into the night and stared at the pool. As many times as I rehashed the story in my mind, I couldn't find any holes. Lo Hui would have complete access to Amalgamated Sureties company history. What bothered me was the distinct possibility Ariana might have ordered each of the deaths in order to sustain herself and her company. That was not too far from the original theory. Nor was a corollary theory of mine, formulated minutes ago: Lo Hui was covering for Ariana.

Still within my own thoughts, I suddenly focused on the narrow trail. Ariana moved slowly in a sheer aqua gown that revealed the outlines of her well formed body and caused me to stand. She advanced as the perfect reincarnation of some long lost dream and said nothing as she approached the open door. The same powerful scent radiated outward as she stopped and slowly unwrapped the sheer fabric. Whatever game she was playing as she stripped naked was enough to dazzle my rationality.

"I don't think this is a good idea," I said, not really caring if it was a bad idea.

She rubbed her smooth skin over my open shirt and her fragrance sunk through my clothes. The lights dimmed and she peeled back my shirt. I didn't care whether Lo Hui killed Rapp or the others. I only wanted her as she undressed me and brought me into bed. I no longer had thoughts, only feelings, touched so intensely and deeply as when we were in the Barsoom Dome and I then was convinced our life together was just commencing.

* * * *

Birds chirping in the outside bushes awakened me near dawn. I pulled the covers over my bare shoulders and turned to my right. Ariana was not in bed and I sat up. I looked outside, toward the burgeoning light across the pool tiles back to the estate.

"Ariana," I said as I leaped from the bed and checked the bath. "Ariana?"

I was caught in the mix of emotions, torn between her sensual intoxication and the stark reality of her absence. The cool air touched my skin as I rushed onto the pool tiles. I called her name several times. The many levels of the house were terraced into the shadows along the hill. Now my cynical disposition cut through the illusions of only a few hours before. I quickly dressed, ran out of the guesthouse and trotted up the narrow path where she had seductively appeared in the accented light. Now I felt conned. I wasn't sure why or how exactly she conned me, but she was gone and my thoughts were scattered. Maybe she wanted me one last time.

"Ariana! Ariana!"

One of the servants in the kitchen looked up from the long counter. "Sir."

"Where is Ariana?"

"I do not know the answer to that question," she said, still holding a stainless steel bowl filled with strawberries.

"Then find some one who can answer the question."

"Yes, sir."

I grit my teeth and kicked the cabinet as she left. Ariana had only wanted me one final time before she disappeared. I leaned against the counter and gripped the edge. Maybe all the other emotions had skewed my thinking. Why would she leave? I was overreacting. She probably had just returned to the house and she would have breakfast with me shortly.

An older woman moved into the kitchen with the girl.

"Mr. Cobb, we thought Miss Cervantes was, well, frankly, down with you in the guest house."

"No, she isn't there. I want an outside zip."

"I don't think Miss Cervantes has opened up those channels to you."

I raised my voice this time. "Listen, you find somebody you can open up a zip right now or there is going to be trouble."

"Yes, sir."

The young lady stared at me and I turned to the window. Platinum City was now orange in the now morning light. Ariana could have let them kill me back on the ledge. I clenched my fists and awaited a logical explanation. I recognized one of the servants from diner. "I have your zip, sir."

"Okay, where is Ariana?"

"She left the estate by tracer about an hour and a half ago."

My heart pounded. "Where did she go?"

"I don't know, sir," he said, handing the zip to me.

"Great." I stared at my zip and speculated whether someone had scanned the contents.

I pushed the first memo. "Harry, this is Max. We managed to determine Lebel was fired by Cervantes when they discovered what he was doing with the policies. Cervantes tried unsuccessfully to convince each of the purchasers, including the late Mr. Rapp, to rewrite their policies. Jody has a summation here."

"Harry, we are looking into a couple of other policies mentioned, but we can delineate the following: Anderson bought his policy on February fourteenth, twenty-five years ago, Burroughs on the twenty-first, Rapp given his on the twenty-fourth. Now, Anderson was killed on June eighteenth. Burroughs, June twenty-second. And Rapp July fourteenth."

Max's voice quickly followed. "And McCann killed on June nineteenth … Harry, Rapp's policy is now six-hundred and nineteen droits. But in ten years it would have escalated to four point one kondroits! Burroughs's policy flies from five thirty-four droits to three point six kondroits! McCann's six ninety six droits to three point five kondroits. You see the pattern. Harry, the pattern is clear. We will get back to you."

Ariana was gone. She had specifically had Miller lie and even alter the policy values. Before I pushed the next memo I walked to the span and viewed Platinum City in the artificial sunlight. The courts could summon Ariana, but in the world of men like Alton Bardsley and Desmond Turcotte, I wasn't so sure Ariana would be liable for anything unless she was implicated in the murders. I sensed all this last night and still succumbed to her advances.

"Harry, this is Renie. I've tried calling you directly and have been told by sources at the Cervantes estate you and spending time with Ariana. It's not my position to monitor your personal life, but would strongly advise against getting involved with her."

"A little late for that, Renie."

I pushed the next memo. "Harry, this is Renie. I've talked to Patenaude extensively about Oakley's death."

"*What?*"

"Apparently the blast wiped out the whole corner of the detention block. I am assuming you know about this. Call me."

I squinted eyes and my stomach soured, not from hunger, but because I was so thoroughly deceived by Ariana, yet she hadn't killed me. And she faked the Patenaude call. Worse, she had used me. I pushed the zip and connected to Renie.

"Harry, I'm in a tracer heading out to the estate."

"She's gone, Renie." I didn't even mention the fake Patenaude message. "She's gone."

"That's okay. I have the accountant, Miller, scheduled to meet me at the hotel restaurant at eleven. I'm convinced he's feeling the pressure and he claims there is a Turcotte link."

"What do you mean?"

"He strongly hinted the problems at IP-5 would mean a prodigious insurance pay-out if they came to light."

"With a company that has limited assets."

"Correct. I'm sure that's why they popped old Oakley." I said nothing as I stared toward Platinum City. Renie's tracer was visible past the hills. "You all right, mate?"

"Ya … She used me one more time is what she did. I'm going to find her, Renie … bring her in."

CHAPTER 19

We waited for Miller at a railing table overlooking the lower avenue. Renie leaned over his ale stein. "Max told me Lebel was unequivocally fired by Mr. Cervantes."

"No other records?" I asked and sipped my jafrin.

"Nope."

"We all know what happened here. So, why aren't the authorities more concerned? I talked to Patenaude no more than fifteen minutes ago. Kranz, Burkhart and the rest of them are doing back flips because their detention cells got wrecked."

"There's more to this than Oakley being shut up, Harry."

"How so?"

"I always look at the end result, mate. This accomplishes two things: It does shut up Oakley about the IP-5 thing, and it diverts attention from the Rapp murder, which further diverts the long chain of murders covering Ariana's financial tail." I nodded and looked down the sidewalk.

"Miller has several zips in his containment case that will verify that if he really is feeling the pressure. Maybe she's threatening him."

"No," I said and fully gulped the jafrin. "That's not it. Miller isn't stupid. He knows we've figured this out."

Renie nodded and raised his hand to the waitress. "Listen, I think we should go back to that estate."

"She's long gone." I stared into my empty jafrin cup and debated whether to have more. Jafrin harmlessly increased alertness and quelled pain, yet my eyes ached. My interest in finding Ariana was not legal, but personal. A crowd gathered near a theater surrounded by clear, lighted bulbs. I leaped out of my seat.

"What is it, Harry?"

"I don't like it." Red security beacons flashed along the avenue, followed by the rapid siren cadence of three white and yellow vehicles. "Let's go."

We raced down the spiral staircase. Renie pushed through the sidewalk stragglers to the congregated mass. I asked several people about the confusion ahead. Somebody claimed a man was dead from a pulser beam, but as we squeezed closer, it was clear the man died from a stabbing outside the theater. I knew Miller was dead from the second I turned on the balcony.

The red uniformed security people hoisted Miller's torso. Slashes covered his neck and face. "Where's his containment case?"

"Good question." Renie pushed up to the stretcher. "This man had a containment case!"

Over the next few minutes, none of the other security people found the case. I backed up against the theater's yellow bricks. "It could take months or years to find out what Miller had in that case. Damn!"

* * * *

Fifteen minutes later, I introduced myself to a Captain Diaz, a young dark-haired, pudgy man. He held a linear zip with a huge blue screen crammed with information. "Gentlemen, here's what we know about the assailant." I heard witnesses interviewed but discounted the bits and pieces I heard. Renie handed me another jafrin cup as Diaz continued. "Oriental man. Five foot nine—"

"Lo Hui …"

"What was that, Mr. Cobb?"

"Lo Hui, Amalgamated employee," I said and swallowed the jafrin still in my mouth. "He killed Miller."

"I've heard that name somewhere." Diaz raised his brows at me. "How do you know this?"

"Guy was following me on Orbitus. Same description."

Diaz nodded and memoed his entire force with Lo Hui's name.

"Why was he following you?"

"I'm involved in an investigation of Amalgamated Sureties."

"I don't need Ariana Cervantes as an enemy," said Diaz, glancing at one of his men. "And Miller, according to his wallet card, also worked for Amalgamated. Why were you investigating Ariana?"

"Murder of policy holders."

"Here?"

"Not that I know of," I said.

"Good. Sergeant, I want a team assembled to interview Ariana Cervantes about this murder."

"Good luck, you won't find her," said Renie.

"Why not?"

I stepped between the two men. "She left early this morning, but I think the estate should be checked … She's gone."

"Then I'll request all ports closed," said Diaz.

"No, I mean she's *gone.* Left Platinum City completely."

Diaz closed his eyes. "We have to check everything."

He ordered checks at all ports and scanned records for very vehicle leaving Platinum City during the past twelve hours. He then boarded a tracer with three of his people, bound for the Cervantes estate. Renie shielded his eyes as the tracer rose upward and we started down the sidewalk.

"Where is Lo Hui?" I asked.

"I have little doubt Mr. Hui will successively evade the security forces."

"Let's get back to the hotel."

* * * *

After dinner, I received a call from Diaz. An extensive search of the Cervantes estate by his men concluded Ariana was indeed gone. All shuttles, extended lines and freighters were on alert for Ariana and Lo Hui, but I was sure they had departed hours ago. Reeling in every craft having departed since this morning was not going to happen.

"I have a definite pattern, beginning three months ago, of repeated trips by Miller to Mars, specifically the Livingston Dome."

"You're whetting my pallet, Captain. Tell me more," I said as Renie worked a zip window at the desk.

"Miller was used as a consultant by Desmond Turcotte. Everyone of his trips required he state his business and destination. Each time, I count fourteen trips, he listed: S. Miller: Turcotte, IP-5."

"Really? I think we have more of a connection to IP-5 activities than we care to know about. How do you think it relates to the murders?"

Diaz dug his fork into a piece of compact nutrient and spoke as he chewed. "Miller was a genius at controlling finances. My guess is he was there to juggle the books. But that isn't the intriguing part. I have a friend, now on lunar duty, whom I talked to about this case. When he was a young recruit on earth he heard of his superiors kicking a guy out of Baltimore named Miller who was told to stop interfering with the settlement of the Samantha Evans' death."

"Come on!" I banged my jafrin cup on the table.

"Samantha Evans' body was never found."

"It gets better. Her brother filed a petition with the court to have Samantha declared dead. The witness to that petition was Ariana Cervantes."

"Wow … Did Miller penetrate the credit, you know, get access?"

Diaz finished the nutrient. "Evans' credit had been transferred six months before to a businessman named—"

"Cauldwell."

"Very good, Cobb."

"He absorbed her credit and Ariana got his estate."

"Probably with Evans' credit intact," said Diaz. "This declaration occurred in the court records in December, 2139. We're considering both Lo Hui and Ariana as hostile to the city."

"That's an understatement."

"I'll talk to you, Cobb. Let me know what you find."

"Thanks for your help, Captain."

"My pleasure."

I turned and Renie spoke as he fiddled with the zip window. "The credit business all makes sense now, Harry. That's why Glut found nothing. And in regard to the Turcotte connection, they brought in Miller to IP-5. It would have cost Ariana a fortune to make good on the corporate loss insurance."

"And Desmond wouldn't give up a dime." I stood and crossed the room. "What about Oakley? How much did he know?"

"He was right in the plant. He knew Miller was around. I'm just not sure who blew up that detention cell."

I sat in the chair next to his window. "Desmond is a lot of things. Master of profit gouging, ill-conceived purveyor of the truth … But I don't list murder as one of his achievements and I've thought about him being peripherally involved in Rapp's murder. Rapp had to die. Ariana had to kill him not only because of his maturing policy, but more importantly, he threatened to expose the IP-5 thing. That's why she went to such great lengths. Well thought out. She had resources for the Evans facial squeeze and was prepared to use the credit if she needed to."

"And you don't think Desmond could have ordered Oakley or Lockheed to kill Rapp?"

"No, Desmond would have paid off Rapp … got him off of Mars. I'm sure Ariana had Rapp in her sights, but when he traveled to pressure Lockheed, she acted quickly. She may have found this out on Orbitus, I don't know. Now, I'm not saying either Oakley or Lockheed, more specifically Oakley, weren't out to get Rapp."

Renie pointed at a yellow, blue lined manifest from Link Transport in the window. "Turcottes own Link. A cash transaction this morning at eight-fifty a.m. I have no way to check whether she called Desmond to get on this flight, but she may have already been cleared."

I looked closer. "No destination. A class-14 transport. Great. Correct me if I'm wrong, but don't you have to file a specific flight plan with the port controller?"

"One would assume that, wouldn't one, mate?"

"Where is that hanger?"

"Port 95, section 11."

"Pack your containment, Renie. We're going for a little trip."

CHAPTER 20

Jody rattled off two additional policy numbers in direct sequence with Rapp's policy. "You're telling me there are two more murders?" I exclaimed as Renie and I moved upward in port ninety-five's elevator.

"A Susan Kraft. Dead by pinpoint. May 23rd. Baltimore. Six days later on Moon Base Graduate, Kathleen Cronin, formerly of Baltimore, was killed by a pinpoint."

"She sounds like a pre-played disk," said Max. "Harry, with your permission, we're heading back to Orbitus. It doesn't matter at this point if there are more pinpoint deaths."

"Sadie will transfer credits to your accounts."

"Sounds like you've nailed Ariana."

I raised my brows and looked straight up through the elevator to the port. "That may be true, Max, but now we have to find her."

"Anything we can do?" asked Max.

"Not at this point."

"Harry, be careful."

"I'm sure *he* will, mate," said Renie.

"You, I don't ever worry about, Ren. Watch Harry."

"Yes, sir." Renie saluted and I cut the zip a few seconds later.

I looked into Renie's blue eyes. "I think I know where she went."

His head tilted slightly. "Where?"

"The Barsoom Dome on Mars."

"How do you know that?"

"I'm not sure. I just know ..."

* * * *

We argued with three lower level management types for closer to an hour. They moved to the upper offices above the hanger only after I called Diaz and told him I was pursuing the lead. The manager of the Link facility was impressed when Renie showed him a Craft Certification License. "A CCL, Level A. Very good. Very good. What can we do for you men?"

"Ariana Cervantes, did she rent a vessel this morning at eight-fifty a.m., Mr. Dill?"

"Precise. I like that." Dill shook his bald head. "I certainly would have remembered that. Miss Cervantes and her father used various private crafts over the years."

"Does the name, Lo Hui mean anything to you, Mr. Dill?" I asked, gazing through the silcoplast to the vast array of white and blue trimmed vessels around the hanger.

"No, sir." He leaned over the zip window and brought up the manifest Renie had found. "Paid in kondroits to a numbered account … I will have to check with the duty officer."

"No destination cleared with the port controller?"

"Odd," said Dill, crunching his light skin. "Get me Officer Potts."

I studied the decals on the curved wingspans below as maintenance people worked on the ships. Potts, from a location somewhere in the city, moved toward the window scanner.

"Craig."

"Potts, this morning. Who paid cash for the use of Link vessel 72273?"

"I didn't handle it."

"There is no flight plan and no certification of pilot," said Dill sternly.

"Sir, I don't know anything about it. I didn't authorize anything. The only way that vessel would get outside the hanger and space bound is from a system override. We didn't. That vessel was on hanger D. Those ships are only used for documents or light transport and not very often."

I looked at Renie. "That's it."

"It's possible, Harry."

"We need a ship to get us to Mars quickly," I said, knowing my thought about the Barsoom Dome was only a guess and a rather prejudicial one. Letting Patenaude know about my suspicion was prudent, but I wanted to talk with Ariana first. She would assume a defensive position should Kranz and his men become involved. "Can we get a ship, Mr. Dill?"

"With the proper credit it"

"We have the proper credit," said Renie.

I feared a scan of my own credit might alert the parent company and eventually Desmond Turcotte. His complicity in this affair irritated me, but shrunk in comparison with Ariana's betrayal.

"We will give you a small Covair Series IX. We have three ships in hanger seventeen. I'll begin preparations. We can have you out of here within the hour."

"Good, the sooner the better."

* * * *

With Renie at the pilot's controls, I spoke with Patenaude as we prepared to leave the inner locks. I peered out the small silcoplast openings up front and then back at Patenaude. "Jahn, I'm trying to tell you Ariana is up to her eyeballs in this."

"That's not the way Burkhart and Kranz see it. They've brought Stanton in concerning the detention cell blast."

"Oh, come on. Ed Stanton wouldn't get involved with anything like this. I don't care how much Desmond pressured him. But that isn't the problem here. You've read the memos I sent about the policies, Jahn."

"Where is she now?"

"We don't exactly know … I have a few ideas."

Patenaude rubbed his lips. "I can tell you right now, Burkhart is under pressure from Commissar Nevis. We have to solve this so people don't think—"

"We're talking about mass murder, Jahn."

"It will have to wait."

"That makes no sense," I said and rolled my eyes as Renie brought the little ship forward. "What do I have to do to convince you?"

"Not me, them … You'd have to link her to the blast."

"I have no evidence for that. I'll talk to you later, Jahn."

"Harry, I would just back off and let us approach this in due time."

I shook my head. "I can't back off, Jahn. There's just too much at take for me personally."

"I understand. Be careful."

"Jahn, you always tell me that."

"And I mean it. Be careful."

"Sure."

I leaned back in the recliner once I closed the zip window. I discounted Ariana's direct involvement in Oakley's death only because she had no direct stake in his demise. Even if Oakley threatened to reveal her and Miller's involvement in IP-5, I doubted she personally planted a bomb."

"I have to file the flight plan now, Harry," said Renie, the zip cap around his head. "Should I list the Barsoom Dome? I'll take the heat if you want me to list some other place."

"No. List Barsoom."

"How can you be sure she's there? There's thousand other places she could hide."

"I just know she's there, Renie.

* * * *

With my eyes covered and the ship humming through space, I forgot about the murders and thought about the time I spent with her last night. I jettisoned my anger at her pathological desire to have the upper hand. I even let my mind drift back ten years when I still worked for the Bureau. The Divone connections to illicit activity in Livingston was the hot topic back then and we were two years into a deep penetration of the family. I was pleased to receive an invitation to Commissar-Elect, Tom Wilson's party at the Commissar's residence in the north dome. A social event of this magnitude provided status and the ability to connect to those with power. Desmond Turcotte arrived with his father and brother, and Constantine Cervantes gave the keynote speech.

Cervantes was accompanied by his thirty-two year old daughter. I first saw Ariana when she climbed the stairs to the main table. Nothing about that night ever left my memory. She graciously swayed in her red satin dress. Her shoulders and arms were smooth white and her hair long, dark and straight. I was taken aback with the sheen of the fabric flowing over her perfectly shaped back. Her father gently kissed her hand and seated her before the long, sea green linen tablecloth. The gold-rimmed wall clock with the stark black Roman numerals chimed nine times. Her eyes caught mine and I wasn't quite sure why she stared at me so long.

Cervantes delivered a dramatic, inspiring speech with the sole purpose of chiding the authorities about taxation. Twice during that speech, Ariana gazed up from her meal and again her eyes met mine. I was a little uneasy and did not want to appear obvious. I found her ambiance, not just her natural beauty, extraordinary. Other men probably sensed what I felt as they hovered around her all night.

She didn't look back when she left with Cervantes and the guests, nor did I think I would see her again. I walked with my Bureau supervisor, John O'Neil, to the main residence terrace. Through the years, I had made contacts around the inner solar system, mostly governmental officials and cops. For the next few hours, I had a wonderful time meeting old friends and played poker for a short time in an upper room with three cadets from The Acre on the Silburn Colony.

I left the game with six droits at eleven-thirty. John had earlier mentioned hitting several bars downtown and I descended the second floor stairs but never found him. Ariana Cervantes gracefully ascended the stairs. She smiled and held my wrist as if she had known me for years. "Can you believe the range of people at this party?"

I wasn't sure whether she was insulting me and still don't know. "You are Ariana Cervantes."

"And you?"

"Harry Cobb, I'm a Special Forces agent with the Bureau."

"I could tell. You have that military forcefulness. It stands out, you know. You have a certain deliberate nature and I know what it takes to become a Special Forces agent."

"Well, I wouldn't make it into something it isn't."

"You put your life on the line in special forces. Tell me, Mr. Cobb, how do you go about investigating those who break the law?"

"With a certain deliberate nature."

She laughed loud enough to pull me up the stairs. "Do you really know who I am?"

"I do."

"People are usually afraid to say boo to me because I'm Constantine Cervantes's daughter."

"Boo," I said as we reached the top of the stairs. Maybe the three ales I had at the poker table made me braver, but there was something more than her beauty and charm. Ariana had the ability to put me at ease.

"Are you always this crass with your female friends?" she asked with a grin.

"I'll check when I get back to my harem."

"I would be willing to bet, Mr. Cobb, you are rather discreet in your dealings."

"Oh, really?"

She still held my arm and we reached an arch open to a small-railed balcony, overlooking the Livingston basin lights.

"Yes, you, Mr. Cobb are a man consumed with right and wrong, driven by a quest for justice and a sense of fair play. And you are not married."

"No, I'm not." She leaned on the balcony railing, but looked at me intently with her dark eyes. "I haven't had time in my career for commitment."

"Commitment is a weight around your neck."

"That's a brutal statement. Commitment works when you're ready." She smiled as if she didn't believe a word of what I said. We talked for close to an hour and then she faced me. "You want to walk the rim?"

I looked upward where the stars ended at a darkened base around the extensive dome. "The rim is for lovers."

She looked over her shoulder, smiled and did not make eye contact. I sensed she admired my directness. "Then I suggest, Mr. Cobb," she said as she turned. "We explore the rim.

* * * *

The dull orange light from the control panel shone across Renie's face. I folded my arms and studied Mars, rusty and bright against the stars. Several times Renie alluded to the fact that the trip to the Barsoom Dome was a fool's errand, but I strongly believed Ariana understood things were collapsing. The authorities and I both knew the facts. Why had she had spared me back at the Cervantes estate? I wanted to believe on some level she cared about me, but reality suggested a more brutal game. She would never extricate herself from the trappings of a high-powered life nor would she control her murderous impulses to maintain that life.

As we remained on course to Mars I finally realized that I didn't care about her failings. I lost myself to her on the Livingston rim ten years ago. Back then, she wore a dark velvet cloak because of the winds at that higher level. With my credit scanned to five droits, I took her hand and we stepped onto the glowing green pathway, nine hundred meters above ground level. A few stragglers meandered along the pathway ahead. I checked the entry-level number, took her hand and we walked along the curved, luminous rail.

I was as much stunned at her ability to personally connect as I was captivated by her radiance and natural beauty. The valley was more prominent once we reached the darkened overlook, extending a hundred meters away from the main rim and lit only by small circular white lights along the base. We talked about inconsequential things as the flags flapped above us. I don't know when exactly I kissed her, but I do remember her lips were sensual. I held her compact body against me and hardly believed I had the most beautiful woman at the party in my arms.

"Harry," said Renie, breaking my concentration.

"Sir …"

"We're going to start entry braking in two minutes." I pulled the retraining harness across my chest. "You all right?"

"Sure."

"The hardest people to figure out, mate, are those who can't get out of their own way, stuck in what they have to do. You see both sides of those people … Which side do you believe?"

"The side you're with …"

I stared at the planet's dusty brown shell. In my heart, I wanted to see that sensuous woman in the Cervantes estate's upper bedroom. That part was only a component. She left the Barsoom Dome because she could only sporadically relate to me in an easy and powerful way.

In less than an hour the dome's jagged peaks and dense green tropical fauna would cover a transformed portion of Vallis Marineris. Ten years ago, when I brought one of the dome tracers over the chateau, I first saw the long water sheets, cascading into the Montero Gorge.

I thought back to on the Livingston rim and how I was astounded when she suggested we travel to the dome for several days away together. I suspected she had frequented the dome, but I didn't care. She had the ability to focus back then and she made me feel as if I were the only other person in the universe.

During the next four nights in the Barsoom Dome, we made love in the airy chateau bedroom and spent our days in terrain gear, hiking the gorge. In my entire life, I had never shared such intense, passionate time with another person. I read her poetry watched old show musicals on the zip window. We even alluded to marriage, but concerns about my career and her extensive social life as well as her position within her father's company, stifled future plans. I was in love with her deeply and completely, and didn't care about my job with the bureau or any future consideration without her.

Then, one morning she was gone just as she was gone from the estate bedroom. I remember the dome was cloudy from a thick dust storm raging outside. Her departure was premeditated because she left a brief memo on the chateau window, formulated, according to the time charter, days before.

As Renie brought the craft around, I unclipped my zip and placed in a code only I knew. Ariana's frozen image filled my zip window. Ten years hadn't changed her that much. She wore olive terrain fatigues and her eyes moistened as she prepared to tell me she was leaving me alone inside the Barsoom Dome. Her voice was smooth and I thought I heard it sandwiched between the air currents rising from the gorge. "Harry, I'm sorry, but I can't stay here. If I do stay here my life will change, veer off in a direction of bliss. I don't discount that and I want that bliss, but please understand I would always be tugged at and that, my love, isn't fair to you."

Her dark eyes overflowed as she sniffled and looked toward the Gondola falls in the gorge. Goose bumps stood on my arms every time I watched the playback. I pressed my lips, hit the zip power button and focused on the planet now filling the forward cabin's clear silcoplast span. I inhaled, and even though I was aware of the horrendous death trail in her wake, I wanted her safe. With the proper representation, I could have her committed to a residential detention colony. She would never leave, but at least she would avoid execution.

CHAPTER 21

Renie said nothing when I played back Ariana's departure. We were in the upper atmosphere and I spotted another dust storm in proximity of the Barsoom Dome, near Thansus Tholus in Xanthe Terra, but west of the sculptured caldera of the dominating Olympus Mons. Renie raised his brows. "You sure you want to do this, Harry?"

I checked images of the dome on the forward window, but through the silcoplast, my eyes traced the actual view of Valles Marineris, cracked and shadowed deep, thousands of kilometers into the brown crust. The rounded reflection of the Barsoom Dome was wedged in one of the venous canyons. With no scheduled flight plan or announcement of destination, Ariana's presence in the dome was questionable, but I had no doubt she was inside. "We're bringing her in, Renie."

"Okay, but we'd better be armed. "I looked back at him.

"This vessel has three pulser rifles in the locked cabinet to your left."

I looked at the closed metal wall. "You think Lo Hui's with her, don't you?"

"Yup."

"I thought about that."

"Why is she here? I mean if she *really is* here," said Renie.

I pinched my lower lip. "Figuring out a way out of this where nobody would look for her. Nobody except me. Maybe she knows I'll follow her and is waiting with her henchman."

"She could have killed you at the estate. My guess, she hopes you don't figure out wherever she is. They stay here for a few days and then disappear."

I nodded and had him open the cabinet. As we reached the lower levels, I grabbed all three rifles, checked the power levels, and sat in my recliner. I let one rifle rest over my lap and prayed she would come willingly.

Renie touched the zip control pad. "Barsoom Dome, this is Covair vessel-1465."

"You are on our window, 1465."

"Permission to enter outside port."

"Show you credit status," said the voice on the other end. Renie placed his palm on a scanner. "Do you wish accommodations, Mr. Coburn? And your flight plan lists a Mr. Harry Cobb."

I placed my palm on a scanner. "Mr. Coburn and I would request only hiking status. In the area of the Montero Gorge."

"We sell our terrestrial activities in six hour blocks and limited to thirty square kilometers. Anything time overage will be docked to your credit as will any retrieval expenses."

"I understand."

"Mr. Colburn is cleared to enter port 14."

"Thank you," said Renie. "Harry, they'll check the pulsers."

"We have pulser rights. They would have seen that in the credit scans."

"Are there shooting ranges here?" asked Renie.

"Yes, there are a few ranges."

"We'll have to stipulate our usage to the ranges and if we get caught firing off range, we'd lose all pulse privileges and risk detention time."

"I really don't give a damn."

Renie grinned and looked ahead. "I like that kind of talk." The craft leveled and hit a few minor air currents. I gripped the rifle and ran the point over my knee. "Harry, I'm the last one to follow the rules, but maybe we should pressure Patenaude again."

"You're talking six hours by conventional tracer from Livingston. I did my duty. I told him. What more can I do? I'm bringing her out of here myself."

* * * *

Port 14 was nothing more than an enhanced silcoplast conduit tube leading into surrounds and the central taxiing area. Workers in amber uniforms directed vessels into wide bays along the open area just as I remembered from ten years ago. The other crafts looked like boats lined up in a marina. I threw one of the rifles to Renie once we were safely inside. He flipped the overhead hatch and the moist dome air flowed into our ship. We stepped onto the silcoplast dock and followed the yellow line to the wide escalator down front.

I gazed up at the white hebon tubes and the high gray silcoplast walls as I did when Ariana and I had arrived so long ago. The humidity hadn't changed, nor had the brightness and hint of foliage at the top of the escalator. I longed for those simple four days and cringed at what I now needed to do.

We walked to the ranger station, a small silver geodesic dome at the end of a long road leading to the mountains. Staff in brown and olive fatigues darted around a visitor's center under a massive map. I studied the dome's inner views within the wall windows as I headed for the accommodations desk and placed my hand on the scanner.

"Hello, Mr. Cobb," said the young woman behind the counter as my credit image appeared on the counter window.

I checked her identification pin. "Good morning, Miss Peters. At least I think, it's morning here."

"You're traveling from Platinum City. You must be tired. We can provide you with a temporary habitat."

I shook my head as Renie joined me. She smiled. "And Mr. Colburn. Pleasure to see you."

"Thank you," said Renie, still looking around the voluminous dome station.

"Miss Peters," I said, leaning on the counter. "I was supposed to meet an Ariana Cervantes and a Samantha Evans here in the dome, but I'm not quite sure if they went to Montero Gorge or somewhere else."

She checked the window and shook her head. "I'm sorry, Mr. Cobb. I don't see any record of either woman nor any reservations."

"What about a Lo Hui?" asked Renie, looking back.

"No, sir."

I removed my zip. "I do have a zip image of Miss Cervantes." She nodded and I brought a general image of Ariana onto the zip. The counter scanner produced a red beam over my window. Three beeps sounded. "Anything?"

"Nothing … I do have past records, but that is confidential." Then she smiled. "Unless she traveled in disguise."

"You may not be too far from the truth, young lady. But if she's not here, who is at the Montero chateau?"

"I can only tell you an elderly couple reserved the chateau six months ago."

"Anybody else in the gorge?" I asked.

"Sure, ten or fifteen people hiking." I shook my head as she raised her brows. "Now, you two wish to hike the gorge?"

"Correct," I answered, still convinced Ariana had entered the dome.

"Clothing to your specifications, provisions and any additional zips are located in transition station five." She pointed across the dome. "You move to the transparent corridor. Transition stations are located down the ramps."

"Thank you. I would request to be notified on my zip should Miss Cervantes, Miss Evans, or Lo Hui arrive at the dome."

"Of course."

I turned and walked briskly past a three-dimensional model of the dome. Old feelings jumbled amidst a creeping disgust. Renie quickly caught up with me. "Harry, I don't think she's here."

"She's here and she's at Montero."

* * * *

Less than an hour later a tracer operator brought us, along with a dozen other people, into the dome's blue sky. Flashbacks crossed my thoughts like the mountain peaks and treetops below. I longed for the serene time, when the Gondola Falls majestically showered long wispy water sheets over the angled mountain rocks. The chateau's brown A-frame, was nestled within thick tropical brush atop the knoll, shone bright in the sunshine. Across the deep gorge, the long rope bridge connected to the distant lake further up the plateau. Trying not to think about my fear of heights, I gazed almost a kilometer down to the winding river along the valley floor. The tracer set down in a clearing between the gorge and the chateau.

I placed my pack over my shoulders and wandered into the tall grass. The timeless chateau beckoned in the dense air and the ever-present sound of cascading water echoed into the canyon. I could see Renie in the corner of my eye. "Where are we headed, mate?"

"Let's check zip frequencies."

"You really think she'll answer?"

"I don't know ..." I took out my zip, but waited until the tracer lifted off. The air was soon still and then birds chirped and a few insects buzzed within the sound of the tumbling falls. I moved directly to the edge of the rocks. "Ariana, this is Harry. I need you to call me."

Renie glanced at me and then into the canyon. I could tell he believed we had spent time traveling from Platinum City for nothing. He took out a nutrient supplement from his pack.

"This place has en effect on you, I can say that."

"Ariana, you left me alone … *again.*"

"I'd bet it's an eight hour trek down to the river. I could use a good bout in the wilderness."

I squinted in the sun over the peaks when the channel hissed. "Harry, *why* did you follow me?"

"Ariana, where are you? Where in the dome?" The channel hiss persisted. "Ariana."

Renie's lips turned downward. "I'll be damned."

"Harry, go … leave and don't ever look back."

"Tell me where you are." The frequency modulated.

"Ariana! Ariana!"

"She ain't gonna tell ya."

"Ariana!" As I paced the rocks, I shouted and hit the zip several times. "You have to answer me!"

I instructed the zip to find the signal coordinates, but the window flashed with a red letters telling me her signal was scrambled. Renie leaned over my shoulder. "I'm surprised she called you."

"Where the hell is she?" My zip beeped. "Cobb."

"Mr. Cobb, this is Steven Foley at the dome ranger station."

"Yes."

"I thought you might want to know, an Inspector Patenaude is less than two hours away. He requested a records check to see if you and Mr. Colburn entered the dome."

"What else did he say?"

"It would appear he's looking for Miss Cervantes just like you."

"Thank you." I stared into Renie's blue eyes. "Jahn is a good man."

"I would rather be dealing with Jahn Patenaude than Kranz."

"Me, too."

* * * *

The canyon bridge wasn't really rope at all, although it appeared that way. Three thick steel suspension cables supported the lower frame. Simulated wood planks formed a long runway, bowing over the chasm, and when the wind hit right or when other people were on the structure, it swayed. I had no fear as I leaned on the ropes and watched the afternoon shadows play games along the distant brown canyon walls. "Why won't she answer? It's been an hour."

Renie still held the pulser rifle with both hands and occasionally checked the rock cliffs through the directionals. "I don't like being out here, mate. We're sitting ducks on this bridge."

"She could have killed me before."

Renie leaned forward. "I hope that cable isn't made from Turcotte steel processed at IP-5."

"I'll second that," I said as I moved along the planks and dreamed back. Ariana and I constantly used this bridge between the chateau and the mountains. "I want to bring her back alive, Renie." I against opened my zip channel. "Ariana ... Ariana ..."

"No hiss. Nothing." Renie looked beyond the trees roots winding through the hillside vines and up to the chateau's diamond windows. "We'd better approach this militarily and not nostalgically."

"You're right."

We held our weapons up, scrambled up the vines and took positions behind the trees. Renie moved out first and pressed his body along the white stucco as I covered for him. I followed him inside as he swung around and kicked the door. The sweet smell of the aged wooden beams and the solid floor skewed my senses. I gazed across the empty room, upward to the bed in the second floor loft and the wide gold framed painting of a dark haired woman with luminous skin, a duplicate of a Rembrandt, as unchanged as the day I walked out of the chateau alone.

Renie tightened his eyes. "Sorry, Harry."

"You mean because she isn't here or because of what was once here?"

"Both."

Even the flowery wallpaper, bursts of color against an off-white background, was the same, and the wide floorboards were warped just as when I crossed the wood barefoot so many years ago. With a tightness in my throat I walked by the stone fireplace. The cold charcoal pieces were scattered under the rusted metal grate and the thick diamonds panes cast the dim late afternoon light across the braided rug.

"It's going to be tough for her to escape with your having alerted everybody."

I checked the time on my zip. "Jahn will be here in less than half an hour."

I sat on a thin bench under more diamond panes and I caught sight of the falls through the thick, wavering glass. The perpetual roar was less pronounced in the chateau, except in the silence of night. I could almost feet her warm body under the sheets, but my longing festered and soon blended into anger, housed in my crunched jaw.

"We need to draw her out," said Renie.

"Ariana, Ariana you need to come out. I'm at the chateau."

"I don't know if it was a good idea telling her that, Harry.

"Security is on the way. Don't turn this into a shoot-out." I looked at my zip and then out the glass. The bridge was clear and the shadows sharper along the canyon. "Damn, I can't believe it's come down to this."

Renie pushed back the blue-checkered curtain by the worn wooden table. "We could look all day and night."

"I understand."

Renie creased his brow. "Ya."

My zip hissed again. "Harry … I'm so sorry."

I grabbed the zip and spun on the bench. "Ariana, where are you?"

"I never understood my demons, Harry … I was trapped."

I walked across the floorboards. "Come up to the chateau. I'll get you out of here and get you representation. I promise. I have connections in the Bureau I can call in."

"I won't spend my days in as a detention colony."

"You have no choice. You could be executed. Come up to the chateau." Renie signaled me and ran over with his zip. The signal was no longer scrambled and emanated from a tower near the falls. Renie and I both headed out the open side door. "Did you hear what I said?"

"I'm sorry you had to become involved in this."

I gazed across the canyon, but didn't see the orange metal tower until Renie handed the directionals to me. "Let's get you out of here before security arrives."

"I'll always love you, Harry."

Renie winced at that remark and we edged our way through the hill vines to the stone stairs. He called me from behind one of the spreading trees. "Harry, treat this as a hostile situation. Please." I nodded but walked toward the rock escarpment. "We get on that bridge and we're open targets!"

"I have to do what I have to do."

"She's a murderer, damn it!"

I said nothing but fully believed she would not fire on me. The sunlight burst across my face as I emerged from the grove into the rock clearing. The orange tower was barely visible near the falls. "Ariana, I going to cross the bridge."

The channel crackled and I grasped my hand around the bridge's twisted rope. I walked directly onto the wood planks. Renie remained behind the tree, and then he scurried down the stone stairs. I was a few hundred meters onto the bridge, closer to the far side, when the air whooshed and buzzed with a bright red pulser beam. I turned back to the chateau and dove onto my stomach. Renie was on his back and holding his chest.

"Ariana, What are you doing?"

A deep, accented voice filled my channel. "You are a fool."

"And you're a son of a bitch, Lo!" With my teeth grinding, I fired my pulser rifle toward the tower. "I'll kill you!"

"You will kill no one, Mr. Cobb. You should have stayed away from her." Another beam shot from the cliffs but not at me. The bridge shook. He fired again and the entire bridge lurched toward the canyon. "Good-bye, Mr. Cobb."

My heart raced as I braced myself against the rope and faced the gorge thousands of meters below. I aimed my rifle at the tower, but soon realized I had no sights on the rifle and would be wasting the power levels. I slowly turned and pulled myself along the ropes. Renie lay motionless across the rocks. The air parted and again vibrated with more pulses. This time Lo hit the bridge underpinnings directly.

I gripped the ropes tightly and my rifle careened into the canyon when the bridge supports snapped. The air pushed by and I had the sensation of swinging through the air on a cadet obstacle course at The Acre. I was soon vertical to the river. Above me, the cables and underpinnings creaked and the structure cracked as it smashed into the rocks. Somehow, I held onto the ropes, but my legs now dangled almost a kilometer above the rock canyon.

My zip, still clipped to my belt, hissed. "I'm so sorry, Harry."

"Go to hell, will you!" I shouted into the whipping air currents.

I peered at least a hundred meters up the ropes and tried not to look into the canyon. My survival would depend upon wedging my feet into the collapsed ropes and using the loops as a ladder to the top. In my younger years, my upper body strength would have allowed me to easily scale lofty trees, sagging ropes and obstacle walls. With added weight and passing years, my ability to hoist my own torso upward only a few feet was now in question.

I lifted my right foot into one of the rope knots, steadying myself as the wind swayed the bridge over the exposed rocks. Across the canyon I wondered if Renie was still alive after Lo Hui's brutal pulser attack. I grabbed another rope circle and stuck my left foot in place. Even with Patenaude on the way, I did not believe Lo Hi would let me live. I began my climb up the bridge, moving at a steady pace until my sides ached and my hands were chaffed red.

I was less than fifty meters from the top when I saw Lo point a rifle down range. I saw him aim at the bridge supports and then the pulser's red beam brightened over the canyon. While I did not see Ariana, I wondered why, rather than kill me outright, Lo wanted to see panic. After repeated attempts, he dislodged the pin embedded in the rocks. Then he turned the rifle to the cables. Each twisted strand splintered as I climbed. He fanned the pulser, but he was presently at an angle and unable to find a straight line to me.

My chest heaving, I neared the top of the cliff. I raced against Lo, now running along the rocks. With no weapon, I could not respond to his attacks even if I made it to the top. He disappeared behind rows of trees and I froze about twenty meters from the frayed cable strands. Another strand broke apart and the bridge pivoted on the remaining strand like a clock pendulum. The wind pummeled my clothes and I scraped against the rocks as I clutched the rope.

I heard Lo's voice from above when the bridge finally swayed to a stop and I faced the jagged rocks. His lunatic dark eyes were fixed on my dangling form and his laugh unraveled my concentration. I turned so my back was against the rocks and away from his line of fire. The distant chateau in the piercing sunlight stirred all the old memories. The sound of Lo's pulser shook my sentimental predilections. He was now trying to pulverize the last cable strand holding the bridge above the gorge. I closed my eyes for a moment and then scanned the cliffs for a new foothold.

Three meters to my right the long sharp rock jutted from under a tiny overhang. I climbed slowly but the bridge buckled again. I was only a few meters back. The strand above me glowed red from the pulser as I grabbed the rock above my right hand, and the full strain of gravity descended onto my chest and shoulders. I stuck my foot into the rock crack and tried not to think of the kilometer drop as the bridge dangled below me.

I managed to get my other hand onto a smaller protrusion and moved closer to the larger angled rock. My eyes watered from the wind and tears cooled on my cheeks as I shadowed the cliffs. The bridge cable cracked and the tremendous weight dragged the structure against the rocks and then into a free fall. I scraped my bloodied hands onto the larger rock. I breathed so rapidly I thought I might fall back.

The canyon currents howled within the steady roar of the falls half a kilometer away. I climbed onto the two-meter extrusion and positioned my buttocks against the rock walls.

"Cobb! Cobb!" Lo was now only ten meters down the other side of the ridge. "You're a clever man, but you're dead!"

Now nothing shielded me from his pulser. I thought about retreating along the rocks, but didn't think I could steady myself without falling. He slowly raised the pulser rifle. I pressed as close as I could against the rocks. I heard another pulser beam, but didn't see it. When I looked up Lo's body tumbled over his rifle. He smacked against the lower rocks and vanished into the canyon.

Ariana, wearing green fatigues, was backlit against the sunlight. "I am so sorry, Harry."

"Shut up!"

"I never meant to hurt you or even get you involved in this."

"I involved myself. We had a future when we were in that chateau ten years ago!"

"Yes ... I hadn't killed anyone then. I hadn't murdered Samantha or killed Henry or my father."

"You what?"

"I killed them all and the policy holders!"

I closed my eyes. "*My God.*"

"And I ordered Lo to kill you on the way to the Excelsior and with the inverted pulser."

"Then why didn't you kill me at the estate?"

"I called off my security people because I knew I was finished. I wanted you one last time. And now it's over." I quickly looked up and she walked closer to the edge. "I must die."

"No, you can be tried as incompetent. You don't have to die."

"On my own level, as convoluted as that was, I loved you, Harry. Everything else in my brain got in the way, but I did and do love you."

I moved on my knees and gripped the upper rocks as she bent her knees. "Ariana, no!"

"I have nothing to live for!"

"No!"

"I'm better off out of your life, my old love. You go on and find love. I know you will."

Before I could respond, she spread her arms like a graceful diver and glided into the air. Her body remained extended and perfectly stable only a few meters over my head, and then she was drawn into the depths. I closed my tearful eyes and pushed my head against the rocks as I closed my fists and cried.

*　*　*　*

The tracer descended in the dim light across the canyon near where Renie had fallen. Red uniformed troopers quickly rushed out the side opening. I was wedged with my knees bent between the rocks and the jutting stone for over two hours. The canyon had darkened and in a short time no one would see me stranded. I wasn't sure whether they were working on Renie or preparing his body for transport. Another tracer appeared above the hills, but crossed above the chateau and over the canyon. Brilliant white hebon spots swept along the canyon walls. I gripped the rocks with my right hand and waved my left hand.

The tracer spent several minutes above the cliffs, but then made a wide arc into the valley. Beams illuminated the snapped cables lines and the burnt rocks to my right and then shone into my eyes. I saw Patenaude in the opening as the craft slowed and gently moved toward me. "Are you all right, Harry?"

I nodded and the wide yellow encapsulated portal moved outward from the tracer opening until it closed off the canyon before me and fit snugly against the cliffs. Patenaude extended his hand and his grip was warm. I moved my cramped legs upward and staggered into the tracer. Emergency personnel surrounded my body with a thermal blanket connected by frequencies to monitors up front.

"Renie … is he …"

"He's still alive."

I closed my eyes and extended my body onto side cot as the tracer retracted the encapsulater. The craft moved away from the cliffs and the wall clicked back into place over the opening. Patenaude leaned over the cot. "Is anyone else out here, Harry?"

I briefly opened my eyes and shook my head. "She's dead, Jahn. She's dead."

Epilogue

Renie, his chest wrapped in a green body wrap for the past two weeks, looked at Max and Jody in the window. "Pulser beam into the ribs, mate."

"How does one take a pulser beam to the ribs?" asked Max.

"On my back."

"You were on your back?" asked Jody.

"He was just being funny," said Max.

"Funny, oh, yes …"

"Forgive my literal friend."

I leaned forward. "I want to thank you both for your work. Uncovering those policies … led to the truth."

"I'm sorry it ended the way it did, Harry."

I nodded and pressed my lips toward the window. "You two take some time off. There's extra kondroits in your accounts."

"What about me?" asked Renie.

"You get another month of rehab."

"You're so kind, mate."

"Is it true what I hear about Desmond Turcotte?" asked Max.

"No fine and no restitution to those having purchased replated steel," I said quickly.

"That doesn't seem fair," said Max.

I gritted my teeth. "Even when they found Kirby's body in the detention cells."

"Sadie says you're going to take some time off, Harry," said Max.

I looked at Patenaude and then back to the window. "I am."

"Then you relax. You be sure and relax."

"I'm a little sick of being stuck high places, but I will relax," I said and stood.

"Yes," said Jody. "Allow yourself to recharge."

"He's not a machine," said Max. "We're going. Honestly, Jody, why don't you take a course in human expressions?"

"Do you think that would be prudent?" she asked.

"See what I have to put up with?"

"You two enjoy each other's company."

The window went blank and I walked slowly from the table. Renie's voice shot out at me. "Where are you going, Harry?"

I heard Patenaude smack his lips. "He's going away, Renie … to get it all out of his system."

* * * *

I was surprised they had already reconstructed the bridge across the canyon. With a backpack and new hiking boots, I trudged up the chateau trail, but I diverted off the trail and up another forested hill. Using a number of old Bureau connections I had Ariana buried on the second knoll. A solitary gray stone rose from the wispy grass furrowing in the canyon wind and the chiseled granite surface was shadowed in the daylight.

I was slated for a ten-day stint at the chateau and would take longer if I needed the time. At the crest, I stared at the gravestone's shadow over the cleared brown soil. I was not a man who relished wallowing in the pain of my past, but I knew the only way to expel the hurt from my soul, was to throw myself into that pain. I would take as long as I needed to work out of the loss and establish new perceptions.

I ran my fingers over the carved letters. As the breezes nudged up the canyon walls and ruffled my hair, I cleared my throat and spoke into the wind.

'She walks in beauty, like the night
    Of cloudless climes and starry skies;
And all that's best of dark and bright
    Meet her aspect and her eyes:
Thus mellowed to that tender light
    Which heaven to gaudy day denies
One shade the more, one ray the less,
    Had half impaired the nameless grace

Which waves in every raven tress,
        Or softly lightens o'er her face;
Where thoughts serenely sweet express
        How pure, how dear their dwelling place.
And on that cheek, and o'er that brow
        So soft, so calm, so eloquent
That smiles that win, the tints that glow,
        But tell of days in goodness spent,
A mind a peace with all below,
        A heart whose love is innocent!'

978-0-595-48534-5
0-595-48534-0

www.ingramcontent.com/pod-product-compliance
Ingram Content Group UK Ltd.
Pitfield, Milton Keynes, MK11 3LW, UK
UKHW041942190726
13854UKWH00004B/1752